WHAT EVERY LORD WANTS

ADELE CLEE

This is a work of fiction. All names, characters, places and incidents are products of the author's imagination. All characters are fictitious and any resemblance to real persons, living or dead, is purely coincidental.

No part of this book may be copied or reproduced in any manner without the author's permission.

What Every Lord Wants
Copyright © 2016 Adele Clee
All rights reserved.
ISBN-13: 978-1-9998938-2-8

The Secret To Your Surrender (excerpt)
Copyright © 2016 Adele Clee
All rights reserved.

Cover designed by Jay Aheer

CHAPTER 1

Prudence Roxbury sat in front of the fire, clutching her embroidery as if it were a prized family heirloom and the bailiff was about to tear it from her grasp.

"Are you listening, Prue?" her sister, Sarah, said with an air of frustration. "Since I mentioned Lord Roxbury's return to Hagley Manor, you've done nothing but stare into the flames. If you don't close your mouth, you will singe your tongue." Sarah chuckled. "Although the thought of you not speaking for a week has appeal."

"You know what this means, Sarah." Prue ignored her sister's comments as shock and disbelief blossomed into excitement. If she hugged her sewing any tighter, she would snap the frame. "It means our prospects have dramatically improved. Now he has found the courage to come home, we will give our relative an opportunity to atone for stealing our house, our furniture, the rug we used to wipe our feet. I bet he's even piddling in my chamber pot. The blighter hasn't an ounce of shame and owes us something for causing such misery."

Sarah shook her head. Her constant tutting sounded like

raindrops dripping onto the windowsill. "We can hardly call a third cousin a relative. I doubt he'll give you a guinea for your trouble. He doesn't even know we exist, so why should he give a hoot for our misfortune? You'll make a fool of yourself if you march over there demanding things you've no right to demand."

"When have you ever known me make demands? I am all a lady should be — quiet and unassuming, kind and affable." Prue chuckled to herself. "Well, I can be when the need arises."

"Which to my mind is not often enough."

"Well, take a long hard look." Prue straightened her back and lifted her chin. "I shall introduce myself as the Lady of Lilac Cottage. I think it has quite an eloquent ring to it, don't you?"

"What about Prudence Pickle from Primrose Cottage? That's far more apt."

They both laughed.

"Imagine the look on his face when I offer a demure curtsy, coo, flutter my lashes and tell him my family call me Pickle."

Sarah put her hand to her chest and shook her head. "Well, if nothing else, it has brought us some amusement this evening."

Prue considered her sister's cheerful countenance. Sarah was far too pretty to sit on a threadbare chair fixing a bonnet fit for a scarecrow. She should dress in fine gowns and have a large house of her own to command. Such a sparkling gem should not hide in a dusty old cottage never to see the light of day.

"You're planning something, aren't you?" Sarah peered at her beneath half-closed lids. "I know that crazed look in your eye, the wild twinkle that spells trouble. You intend to ask Lord Roxbury to sponsor a come out."

"It will hardly be a come out when you're twenty years old. Besides, it will be far too late in the Season, and we can't afford to wait another year. No, I was thinking of a casual introduction into society." Prue's gaze drifted over her sister's golden hair shimmering in the candlelight. What lord wouldn't want such a stunning lady on his arm? "There must be a host of eligible gentlemen seeking a lady with your grace and beauty. Besides, you're the only one not cursed with the hereditary dull, muddy-brown locks and insipid features. You owe it to your siblings to make a good match."

Sarah frowned. "But you've always told me not to settle for anything less than love."

"Well, yes, but that was before the roof started leaking and the butcher put the price of beef up by a farthing a pound." When Sarah looked aghast, Prue added, "I'm joking. You shouldn't settle for anything less. Just pray the gentleman you choose is rich and willing to take care of your poor, destitute sisters."

As if on cue, they heard the patter of bare feet along the hall before the door flew open and Anna and Jayne came rushing into the room.

Prue forced a serious expression. "It's eight o'clock. Shouldn't you both be in bed?" With the girls being age ten and twelve respectively, Prue insisted on a strict routine.

"Grandpapa has fallen asleep in my bed," Anna cried, "and I can't wake him."

"He's snoring again." Jayne stepped forward to offer her support. "It's so loud it sounds like a bear is trapped in his stomach. Oh, can't you come and move him, Pickle?"

Canon fire wouldn't rouse the old man when he was in a mind to sleep. Being the eldest had few advantages it seemed.

"No doubt, he is expecting an imminent attack from a French vessel and has rushed to hide in his cabin." Prue sighed. Their grandfather's overwrought imagination and frequent forgetfulness had resulted in many strange and unexpected situations. His prime motivation was to avoid being captured by the French. And theirs was to make him feel safe and secure at home — a task that proved more difficult by the day.

"I'll come with you," Sarah said. "I'm straining my eyes trying to sew in this light. And after we've settled Grandpapa, I think I'll go to bed."

"That's a splendid idea." Prue needed an early night, too. "I must be as bright as a button when I confront Lord Roxbury tomorrow."

"I'd think twice before charging over there. It will all end in trouble."

"Don't fret." Prue offered a sly smirk. "When have you ever known me to get myself into a pickle?"

∽

After a hectic morning, the two-mile walk to Hagley Manor, passing newly ploughed fields while listening to the birds' joyful chorus, brought a welcome relief. Prue's head was pounding as she had done nothing but toss and turn all night, imagining all the possible scenarios should Lord Roxbury refuse her request. To make matters worse, Grandpapa had dived under the table during breakfast, sending plates and teacups flying. It had taken an hour to settle him, but he seemed happy enough when she'd told him she was going out for reinforcements.

It was close to midday when Prue opened the tall iron gates and followed the path leading up to the manor. The house had been her home for over twenty years, and she wasn't sure how she would feel seeing someone else sitting in her father's chair, reading his books or writing at his desk. Lord Roxbury hadn't been in residence since inheriting two years earlier. People said he favoured the delights of the city, whatever that meant. Although from what she had heard of his father's scandalous past, she could only imagine.

A nervous shiver raced through her.

Sarah was right. It would not do to be forceful or assertive. Neither would it do to appear weak and insipid. She let out a heavy sigh.

Be polite, demure, and confident, she told herself as she strode up to the front portico. But the horrifying sight she witnessed on her approach caused a sudden burst of anger.

"What in heaven's name do you think you're doing?" She raced up to the gentleman piddling in her mother's Grecian urn. Her father purchased the huge planter as a gift and Prue had tended it every year after her mother's death. "Stop that at once! You'll kill the roses."

The gentleman flicked his golden locks from his brow and glanced back over his shoulder to cast an icy stare. Then he fiddled with his breeches and turned around to face her. "What business is it of yours?" He cast a disdainful look over her plain dress and simple bonnet. "Who the hell are you?"

The sickly sweet stench of spirits, mingled with stale tobacco and some other foul smell, flooded her senses. Good heavens. A degenerate, the worst of dissipated scoundrels, was living in her beloved family home.

"It doesn't matter who I am." She did not bother to hide her contempt. All hope of pleading for money and finding someone to sponsor her sister's come out was now dashed. "Besides, I doubt you'd know your own reflection in a looking glass. Now, run inside at once and fetch a jug of water."

The rogue burped and stumbled as he swung back around to stare at the pot.

"Are you doing what I think you're doing?" Prue cried, fearing she had interrupted his flow, and he had not finished his business. And to think she was annoyed at the thought of him using her chamber pot.

"I'll not be told what to do by the hired help," he slurred. "If I want to pee in an urn, I damn well will. Be off with you, wench. Have you no chores to keep you busy?"

That was it. Despite being in dire need of funds, she'd not forsake her principles. Stomping over to stand on the other side of the urn, Prue was relieved to find the fall of the gentleman's breeches still fastened.

Bending over and grasping the rim of the stone planter, she refused to let go. "By all that's holy, I'll not let you do it again. You will have to drag me off this pot."

The gentleman swayed back and forth before grabbing the sides nearest to him. The urn wobbled on the small stone plinth as he gave it a sharp tug. "And what if I refuse?"

Prue pulled it towards her to reinforce her point. "I don't care if I have to stand here until nightfall. I'll not let you ruin my mother's roses."

The gentleman cast a stern glare. "I said let go."

"No!"

"What the devil's going on here?"

Prue glanced back over her shoulder to find another gentleman standing on the steps. With his hands braced on his hips in a rather regal manner, he raised a curious brow.

"Ah, there you are, Roxbury. This chit is attempting to steal your roses. I suggest you call Mrs Harris and have the wench escorted to the nearest asylum for witless females."

So, this was Lord Roxbury.

Relief coursed through her. This gentleman appeared both sane and sober. Confidence radiated from every fibre of his being. Whatever problem she thrust at him, he would know of a way to solve it.

"Thief," the scoundrel whispered.

"One cannot steal their own roses." She gritted her teeth at the vulgar gentleman opposite. Oh, he was the most odious creature she'd ever met. "Perhaps I should have you nailed to the pillory for lewd behaviour and criminal damage."

"And where is your evidence?" He gave a sly smirk. "I see nothing but an abundance of white buds."

"Perhaps when you come back in the morning—"

"Enough!" Lord Roxbury yelled. "Bradbury, get inside and clean yourself up. You look like you've spent the night frolicking in the stables."

"I have," the fellow chuckled. He tugged on the pot once more just to rouse Prue's ire. "I suggest you speak to your staff, Roxbury. Teach the girl here to respect her betters."

"My betters?" Prue said incredulously. "I was not the one piddling in a flower pot."

"Why, girl, I should have you whipped for your insolence."

Lord Roxbury descended the steps like Zeus coming down from his throne to speak to a group of lesser mortals. "On second thoughts, Bradbury, there's no time to tidy your clothes. I'll summon your carriage while you pack your things. I find the country air makes you far too unstable a house guest. And I would hate to embarrass you by pulling you up for shoddy manners."

"What?" Bradbury's cheeks ballooned. "You can't be serious. I was only fooling around with the girl."

"I suggest you hurry so you'll make it back to London before nightfall."

Prue watched the exchange with keen interest. Lord Roxbury was not a man to trifle with and had suddenly risen a notch in her estimations. Indeed, a strange feeling took hold, one too difficult to define. Her chest felt warm; her heart raced, and she could feel it pulsing in her neck. Perhaps it was because she knew her task to outwit him would be far more difficult than she'd anticipated.

"I won't stay where I'm not welcome. I've had my fill of this place, anyway." Bradbury scowled at her as he mounted the steps and stomped inside.

Lord Roxbury gave a weary sigh and brushed a lock of brown hair from his brow. "Please accept my apologies for his crass behaviour." He glanced down at the old dress she had worn to incite his pity. "I heard you mention these were your mother's roses. I assume she works here."

Prue could not blame him for making the obvious assumption. "No, my lord," she said politely, deciding it best to take the respectful approach. "My mother planted these roses, and I tended them every year after her death."

"I see. So your mother used to work here, and now you feel obligated to care for her flowers. I only ask as I have recently taken up residence and am unfamiliar with the comings and goings of my staff."

"You mistake me, my lord." She fought to hold back a sudden surge of emotion. "My parents were Lord and Lady Roxbury, the previous owners of Hagley Manor. These are my mother's flowers. The manor was my family home."

CHAPTER 2

Max Roxbury stood dumbstruck.

The lady standing before him was a distant relative and a complete stranger. If one scoured back through the generations, they shared a family connection, apparently the same surname, but nothing else. Judging by the well of tears brimming in her brown eyes, the house he regarded with casual indifference held a wealth of fond memories for her.

"Would you care to come inside and take tea?" It was the least he could do under the circumstances. He was not a man who enjoyed mindless conversation while sipping the juice of stewed leaves. He preferred something a little more potent, something to heat the blood.

She swallowed, straightened and inhaled to prevent the tears from falling. He found he admired her resilience. Most ladies of his acquaintance would have sobbed to gain sympathy, blubbered as an excuse to feel a strong masculine arm draped around their shoulder.

"Yes, tea would be lovely. If it's no trouble."

Max offered a graceful bow. "It's no trouble," he said in

his usual rich drawl. "After the disrespectful way Bradbury spoke to you, I need to make amends."

Her countenance brightened. When she smiled, something remarkable happened to her face. What some would consider plain and average looking features: lips neither full nor thin, a nose neither elegant nor disproportioned, eyes with no unusual depth of colour, transformed into something spectacular.

"If you wish to make amends, my lord, I do have a proposition for you." Her husky voice caused the hairs at his nape to jump to attention.

Was she aware of the salacious implication her tone aroused? He didn't think so. Many men would take her comment as an invitation to partake in flirtatious banter.

"Now I'm intrigued," he said, although he had been more than fascinated when he found her wrestling with a potted plant. Glancing beyond her shoulder, he asked, "Did you come here alone?"

She nodded. "We live but two miles away. When I heard you had taken up residence, I simply had to come." With a raised brow, she added, "There is no one at home to object. You need not concern yourself with any impropriety. Things are more relaxed in the country. Besides, this used to be my home, and I am acquainted with the staff."

"Of course." The question plaguing him tumbled from his lips. "By your comment, am I to assume you're not married?"

"Me?" She jerked her head back and made an odd puffing sound. "Good heavens, no. Married? No."

Good. A decent husband would not allow his wife to roam the countryside alone, to accost inebriated gentlemen in the hope of saving the roses.

Curiosity burned inside.

Why did she find the thought of marriage ludicrous? Most women were busy plotting and planning ways to trap unsuspecting peers. And it put to rest his earlier assumption that perhaps she'd come to drag a marriage proposal from him.

Max pushed the thought aside. "Then I feel an introduction is long overdue." He straightened his shoulders and bowed. "As you're aware, I am Lord Roxbury. My friends and family call me Max."

"As in Maximillian?" she asked, raising an inquisitive brow.

"Erm, no, as in Maximus. It was my grandfather's name on my mother's side."

"Oh. It is quite an unusual name." She curtsied. "I am Miss Prudence Roxbury. My close friends call me Prue. Sometimes, my sisters call me Pickle although I don't expect you to do the same."

Max failed to suppress his amusement. "Pickle? Why, because you often find yourself in troublesome situations?"

After recent events, he could well believe that.

"No, because I have a fondness for vegetables preserved in vinegar."

Max did laugh then, loud and hearty. But Miss Roxbury's quirky brow led him to believe she was teasing him. "It has nothing to do with either of those things, does it?"

She smiled, and her inner radiance shone through. "No."

There it was again, the glint in her eye, the tempting tone that created an air of mystery he felt forced to pursue. He could not recall the last time he'd met a lady so entertaining and would happily converse with her on the steps for hours.

"Shall we go inside, Miss Pickle?" he said with a grin. "I shall ask Mrs Harris to send someone to water the flowers. And I am eager to hear this intriguing proposition of yours."

"Certainly, my lord."

"We'll discuss the matter in the study," he said as he escorted her into the hall. "I'm sure you know the way."

Guilt flared in his chest when he sat in her father's seat on the opposite side of the desk. With the corners of her mouth curled up into a sweet smile, she glanced around the room with a look of wonder, her gaze lingering on the cabinet filled with leather-bound books.

"Please, browse through them if you wish. I'll call for tea while you wander around."

Her eyes sparkled to life. "You don't mind? I do not wish to intrude."

"No, not at all."

Max watched her rise from the chair, eager to know where she would go first. As expected, she walked over to the cabinet and peered at the books inside. He heard her hum a sweet tune as she tilted her head and perused the collection. The air about the room swirled with a level of intimacy he found highly distracting. Indeed, he could not drag his gaze away from her.

Perhaps the months spent worrying about marriage had addled his brain. No doubt his father thought it amusing to add certain stipulations to his will. Max could almost hear the scoundrel laughing from beyond the grave.

"My father loved to read," she said, disturbing his reverie.

"Looking at his library, I see he had a fondness for Greek philosophy."

She glanced back over her shoulder. "Do you study the subject yourself?"

"There are a few theories to which I can attest. I believe good character is not a matter of parentage but rather a gift from the gods. I believe that to know the father does not necessarily mean one can claim to know the son."

"You mean people should judge us as individuals. It sounds as though you speak from personal experience."

Max shrugged, not knowing why he'd chosen to reveal

something so personal, something he usually kept hidden. "Perhaps I am."

She did not pry as some ladies would do. She did not demand a more thorough explanation but accepted his comment without passing judgement.

Now he found *that* more than fascinating.

With his eyes fixed on her every movement, he watched her walk to the window.

"The view is lovely from here," was all she said before crossing the room. She ran her gloved hands over the wall, across the decorative architrave: a wooden moulding that appeared to frame nothing at all. "Do you mind?"

Max shook his head. "Mind what?"

"If I take a peek in here?"

Struggling to understand her meaning, he said, "Not at all."

With her palms held out in front of her, she placed them flat on the wall and pushed. The quick movement resulted in a clicking sound, and an opening appeared.

"What the blazes?" Max jumped to his feet and rushed over to stand at her side.

She chuckled. "Did you not know there's a secret room?"

"No. I've been in here a handful of times, but none of the staff mentioned a hidden cupboard."

"In years gone by people used it as a pot room, a place to relieve oneself without resorting to piddling in planters." She stepped into the small space. "My father used it as a snug. A place to hide away, to sit and reflect on all the beauty life has to offer."

Max noted the leather wingback chair and the small side table supporting a decanter and glass. The various paintings on the wall were pictures of the same woman. He stepped closer to study them, recognised a vague similarity to Miss Roxbury. "Is this your mother?"

"Yes." She gazed up with a look of admiration. "My father sketched and painted her likeness often."

Max sat in the chair and stared up at the pictures. The room felt like a shrine: a place to worship the love of one's life. A hard lump formed in his throat. His mother had deserved this level of devotion as opposed to the years of humiliation she'd suffered at his father's hands.

Now, he was expected to marry, too, if he had any hope of inheriting everything. History was to be repeated and, like his poor mother, he would be forced to marry for convenience — just as his father had planned.

The cold-hearted bastard could cause misery even from the fiery pits of Hell.

He shot out of the chair, needing to distract his mind from dwelling on the past, on the future, on anything involving matrimony. "Why are they here? Why did you not take them with you?"

"They are part of the inventory. Mr Jameson made it quite clear they were not to be moved."

A sudden wave of sadness washed over him. Never could he recall experiencing such a vast array of emotions all in the space of an hour. He considered how heartbreaking it must be to leave such treasured mementoes behind.

"I shall have them packaged up and delivered to your home," he suddenly said, knowing it was the right thing to do. Good Lord, he truly had gone a little soft in the brain.

She swung around to face him, her eyes wide with shock. "Do … do you mean it?"

"I would never trifle with someone's feelings." The words roused a small pang of guilt for the way he had ended things with Catrina. Besides, why would he want to sit and look at the paintings? They would only remind him of his family's failings.

The smile on Miss Roxbury's face lit up the room. She

placed her hand lightly on his arm as she struggled to contain her excitement. "I cannot thank you enough. When I came here today, I wasn't sure you would receive me. But you have been nothing but considerate and respectful of my position."

The compliment touched him. The hand on his arm caused a strange sense of awareness to course through his body. Surprisingly, he felt mildly aroused.

"I've yet to hear your proposal," he said, hoping conversation would dampen his ardour. "You may change your opinion of me once you've heard my answer. Perhaps we should return to the study and take tea."

Or something a damn sight stronger.

Her gaze drifted over his face, lingered on the dimple on his chin. "You must think me rude for even thinking of asking for anything more. Not after what you have just done. Not after all you've given me."

"Oh, there's plenty I could give you, Miss Roxbury." He jerked his head back, shocked that the words had tumbled from his lips. Why the hell had he said that? And in such a licentious tone. "What I mean is, I am known for my generosity. And your need must be great for you to come here."

He gestured to the room beyond the secret snug, eager to leave the intimate space. She continued to wander about the study, trailing her fingers over books and ornaments while he summoned a maid who alerted Mrs Harris as to the identity of their visitor. It hadn't occurred to him they were acquainted, and he watched her embrace the housekeeper as though they were lifelong friends.

"Forgive me," she said, finally sitting down to drink her tea. "I did not come here to impose."

"So why did you come?" Curiosity burned in his chest.

She sat forward and placed her cup and saucer on the desk. "Well, I will not attempt to preserve my dignity by lying to you. I've come to beg a favour. A very large one. One of monumental proportion."

"Monumental proportion," he repeated languidly. If she wanted something large and impressive, she had come to the right place.

"While we manage from day to day on the allowance provided by my father's estate," she said, oblivious to his amorous mood, "we do not have the funds necessary for ladies' frivolities."

Max could not imagine Miss Roxbury indulging in fanciful whims. She appeared far too practical to fuss over fashions. "You need money for new dresses?"

"Well, yes and no. My younger sister Sarah is an exceptional beauty. I am sure you'll be all agog when you meet her."

"I am not a man who excites easily, Miss Roxbury." Indeed, he had seen more than his fair share of beauties to appear indifferent to their charms. In his experience, a pretty face often masked an insipid character.

"Perhaps, but Sarah is good-natured and kind," she said, sounding like a matron sponsoring a debutante. "The beauty of her character only enhances her fine features."

"What is it you're asking for?" He was starting to feel apprehensive. Did Miss Roxbury want him to offer for her sister? "Surely your monumental request amounts to more than a few dresses."

Miss Roxbury huffed. "Well, if you give me a chance to explain instead of interrupting, I will tell you."

Max pursed his lips. She was extremely amusing, even when angry. "Forgive me. Please continue."

"As I was about to say, Sarah missed her come out as we were mourning our mother's passing and then our father took ill, and well …" She gave an odd little wave. "I'm certain she will be an instant success, but I need your help to fund an event. I need you to find a suitable lady willing to act as her sponsor. An introduction into society is all I ask. I will, of course, contribute in any way I can."

Max sat back in the chair and studied her. It took a tremendous amount of courage to plead for help from the one person you had every right to despise. The money did not pose a problem. But did he want to become entangled in family matters? Then again, they were hardly family. He preferred the company of friends. There were no expectations, no deep feelings of resentment or betrayal when they inevitably let him down.

A knock on the door penetrated the uncomfortable silence.

"Enter."

Mrs Harris appeared in the doorway. "It's Mr Bradbury, my lord. He's leaving. I thought you might want to see him off."

Max shook his head. "No. Let him leave. I have nothing else to say."

His housekeeper nodded and closed the door.

Miss Roxbury cleared her throat. "Do not forsake your friend on my account. I believe I did not help matters with my abrupt manner. And I'm sure he'd been drinking this morning."

"It is of no consequence. I would not allow him to speak to my staff in such a way. Besides, he is not a friend, but merely an acquaintance looking for the means to cure his boredom."

The ease with which he dismissed Bradbury was the reason for his hesitance in helping Miss Roxbury. And with Catrina baying for his blood, he did not need any more complications in his life.

"Well, perhaps it's for the best," she said with a sigh. "I see little sense wasting one's time and effort on those who mean so little to you."

No doubt her family had never disappointed her. He would bet a hundred pounds her parents had been nurturing, supportive, kind and forgiving. When a man loved a woman as deeply as her father had done, those witnessing such a profound emotion probably possessed an inner confidence, a belief that the world was good.

Would spending time in their company alter his rather cynical view of life?

"You do not have to decide now." She stood and tugged at the hem of her jacket. "I shall leave you to consider what I've said."

A strange emptiness filled his chest at the thought of her leaving, which he put down to the distinct lack of stimulating conversation he'd suffered lately.

"I do have one more thing to ask." She winced as though anticipating his response.

He should have found her constant demands irritating, but he didn't. For once in his life, he felt needed. "What is it now?" he said, fearing Miss Roxbury would ride roughshod over him if he did not try to protest. "Don't tell me. You want me to hold a garden party for the whole village, or pay for the repairs to the church roof?"

"Oh, nothing as taxing as that." She smiled at him again, and he made a mental note to do his utmost to make her smile more often. "I would like you to write a note for me. I will dictate."

"What? You want me to write it now?"

"Yes, I would like to take it with me if I may."

The lady knew how to pique a gentleman's interest. "Before I set pen to paper and foolishly sign over everything I own, I would like a brief idea as to the content of the missive."

"Oh, I doubt anyone could fool you, my lord." She sat back down. "I would like you to write a brief message. Something like — *reinforcements are dispatched ... a battalion has intercepted an attack from the French quarter.*"

Max stared at her.

"You can forge a signature," she continued, "as he'll be none the wiser. But use the word *captain* as it will sound more authentic."

Max raised a dubious brow. "You're serious, aren't you?"

"One does not joke about matters of national security." A smile touched Miss Roxbury's lips. "My grandfather lives with us. He has a problem with his memory and still thinks we're at war with France. I told him I was nipping out to bolster reinforcements."

Max raised his chin in acknowledgement. "Ah, I see," he said, although he was still somewhat confused. But as there was nothing incriminating in penning the note, he scrawled away, dusted the paper and folded it before handing it to Miss Roxbury.

"Thank you." She leant forward and grasped the corner of the note between her thumb and forefinger, but Max refused to let go.

"Before you leave, I have already made my decision about whether to help your sister," he said, trying to understand why he had an overwhelming urge to come to her aid.

"Yes?" Her expression conveyed both fear and an eagerness to hear his answer.

"I will agree to provide the funds necessary including an introduction into society, but on one condition."

Her bottom lip trembled, and she tried to disguise it. "I am open to negotiation."

"I suggest we barter services, Miss Roxbury. I do not want you to feel indebted. I will arrange for a dance tutor and a modiste to come from London."

Miss Roxbury's eyes lit up. "How wonderful." But then she narrowed her gaze. "And what do you require in return, my lord?"

Max felt a frisson of excitement course through him as he studied her. Dismissing all salacious thoughts, he said, "I would like you to act as a guide. I know nothing of the house, the surrounding land, or the tenants. For the dance tutor and the dresses, you will owe me two days."

Miss Roxbury stared at him with wide eyes. "You want me to stay here?"

"No, Miss Pickle." He suppressed a chuckle. "I will call for you on Thursday. Once here, you will tell me all about the house, give me a personal tour, and my coachman will take you back home in time for supper." Max released the letter and held out his hand. "Well, are you willing to strike such a bargain?"

Her hesitant gaze wandered over his face, but then she offered her hand. "Very well, my lord. I shall give you two days."

"Excellent," Max replied, trying to ignore the rush of desire the touch of her hand ignited.

CHAPTER 3

THE LOUD COMMOTION DOWNSTAIRS CAPTURED PRUE'S attention. With a heavy sigh, she straightened the coverlet on Anna's bed before heading to the landing and peering over the balustrade.

"What is going on down there?"

Anna appeared at the bottom of the stairs. "Did you call me, Pickle?"

"I thought I heard shouting. Where's Grandpapa?" She'd spent most of the morning hiding behind the curtains armed with a rolling pin, which her grandfather assured her was the rifle he had used to bring down ten grenadiers.

"He's resting in the drawing room."

"Good. Try not to disturb him." With any luck, she could leave the house without explaining where she was going.

Three days had passed since she'd made the deal with Lord Roxbury, yet the memory of the short time spent in his company occupied her thoughts constantly. It was strange how the mind concocted its own version of events. To some extent, she knew how her grandfather felt. To have images thrust into one's head without provocation or reason was baffling.

For the last three nights, she had dreamt about Lord Roxbury. Suffice to say, the amorous images had caused her to wake with a start. She'd spent the early hours suppressing thoughts of warm lips, muscular arms, and an array of other things no innocent female should even comprehend.

Now it was Thursday. And she had no idea how she would look him in the eye without blushing.

Lord Roxbury was kind, considerate, a gentleman of good breeding. All the more reason for her to convince him to marry Sarah. They would make an excellent match, and Prue would love nothing more than to see her sister as mistress of Hagley Manor. It should not be a difficult task. Sarah's undeniable beauty would leave the lord in a tizzy, and her sister would soon see the merits of his excellent character.

Simple.

"Pickle! Pickle!" Anna's shouting disturbed her reverie. "There's a carriage outside."

Good heavens. Was it eleven o'clock already?

"I'm coming." Prue hurried down the stairs as though the chimney stack had caught fire.

"Lord Roxbury is here," Sarah said, almost bumping into her in the hallway. She screwed up her nose as she scanned Prue's faded brown dress. "Please tell me you're not wearing that old thing?"

Prue nodded. While Sarah needed no fancy adornments to attract attention, Prue decided that looking dull and dowdy would only enhance her sister's appeal.

"Quick. You must hurry. There's still time to change," Sarah continued in a mild state of panic. "You can borrow my green dress as it will look so pretty with your hair."

"No, no. You know I prefer comfort over looks."

Jayne came running towards them, her arms flailing.

"Henry is here, too. Henry is here and is about to knock the door."

Henry was now Lord Roxbury's footman and had spent many hours entertaining the younger children over the years.

As soon as Prue opened the door, both Anna and Jayne pushed to the front.

"Henry!" they cried in unison, and the footman tried to keep his back straight and his face expressionless.

"Step away girls," Prue whispered in a stern voice as she did not want to rouse her grandfather. Nor did she want Lord Roxbury to think they lacked breeding by fraternising with the servants. She noted the paper packages in Henry's arms. "At least let him come inside before you harass him."

Both girls shuffled back. Henry bowed and gestured to what was obviously some of her father's paintings.

"Take them into the parlour, Henry," Prue instructed, and Sarah directed him to the room in question.

As Henry moved from the doorway, Prue came face to face with Lord Roxbury. Damn it. Her cheeks flamed as soon as her gaze fell to his sinful lips. She relived the moment in her dream when he asked for two nights of debauchery instead of two days playing nursemaid.

"Miss Roxbury." He inclined his head, his penetrating gaze scanning her from head to toe. "What a pleasure it is to see you again."

"My lord," she said in a bid to compose herself. "W-won't you come in?"

"Thank you, but only for a moment." He stepped into the hall. "We have a prior engagement, as I'm sure you recall."

Only for a moment?

The whole point of her dressing as the destitute relative was to demonstrate her sister's attractive countenance. When he saw Sarah, he would reassess his decision.

"There's no rush, my lord. You can have me for the whole day."

Lord Roxbury coughed into his fist. "What a delightful prospect."

"Would you care to come and meet my sisters?" she asked eagerly, although it wasn't a question. She would drag him into the parlour if forced to do so.

"Of course."

A loud clattering behind her caught his attention, and Prue groaned inwardly.

Lord Roxbury pointed to the room at the end of the hall. "It sounds as though someone's had an accident."

"Oh, pay it no heed." Prue waved her hand dismissively. Her grandfather could ruin everything. "It is probably just the cat. He's forever chasing his tail and knocking things over."

"I thought I heard a man groaning." Lord Roxbury moved to stand at her side as he stared inquisitively at the open door.

"What's all this noise?" Her grandfather rushed out into the hall.

Both Prue and Lord Roxbury jumped at the unexpected sight. The tails of her grandfather's shirt hung over his breeches; hair sprouted from his head in wild tufts and he glared at them while standing in his stocking feet.

"Heaven help us," Prue muttered under her breath. "I shall apologise in advance for his strange antics."

"Who goes there?" Her grandfather narrowed his gaze. Without his spectacles, he was practically blind. He shuffled forward, his eyes growing wide as they settled on Lord Roxbury. "The French!" he yelled. "The French! Run, Pickle."

Without another word, her grandfather charged forward and, with surprising strength, tackled a stunned Lord Roxbury to the floor.

"I'll hold him here, Pickle, while you get the rifle. Shoot the blighter if you have to."

Lord Roxbury coughed and spluttered; the force to his chest had taken the air from his lungs.

"This is Lord Roxbury," she said, grabbing her grandfather's arm and tugging it in an attempt to move him. "He's not fighting for the French. Captain Lawrence sent him here with a message."

The old man pressed his face closer to Lord Roxbury, their noses almost touching. "Good heavens. I thought we were under attack. It's that cravat of yours, far too fancy for an Englishman." He scrambled to his feet and offered the perplexed lord a hand. "Sorry, old boy. One can never be too careful."

Lord Roxbury stood and brushed the dust from his blue coat. "Pay it no mind." He exhaled. The look in his eyes conveyed both amusement and pity. "I understand. These are dangerous times."

"Are you all right?" Prue mouthed silently when his gaze locked with hers.

Lord Roxbury nodded. A smile touched the corners of his mouth, and she breathed a sigh of relief.

"Well," Grandpapa said, leaning in after sneaking a quick glance back over his shoulder. "What news do you have?"

Prue groaned upon noticing the lord's confused expression. "Grandpapa is referring to the message from Captain Lawrence."

Lord Roxbury stared at her, but then turned to her grandfather and said, "The militia have moved to their headquarters in Tonbridge, near the castle. Captain Lawrence said to tell you that the area is secure and that you can sleep easy in your bed."

Grandpapa put his hand on his chest. "Oh, it is a blessing to know they are but a few miles away." With numerous nods, he turned on his heels and withdrew to the drawing room.

"I am so sorry," she said, noting that his hazel eyes appeared warm brown in the dull hallway. "He is a little unstable at times. That is all."

Prue felt a little unstable, too. She feared her weak knees would not support her body. Most gentlemen would have cursed or shown disgust at such reckless behaviour from a man of her grandfather's declining years. Lord Roxbury had shown kindness, understanding, and compassion. Prue's heart skipped a beat. It took an immense amount of effort to suppress the fluttering in her stomach. After all, she could not nurture an affection for her sister's betrothed.

"Next time, I shall come prepared," he said, offering a reassuring smile.

Next time? Thank heavens the whole episode had not dissuaded him from offering his assistance.

They stepped into the small parlour. The children's lively chatter made the room seem crowded and chaotic. What would he think of them?

Prue tugged her sister's arm and swung her around to face the man she would soon marry, if Prue got her way. "My lord, I would like you to meet my sister, Miss Sarah Roxbury."

Lord Roxbury offered a formal bow.

"My lord." Sarah's curtsy was as sophisticated as any lady gracing the ballrooms of London. "May I thank you for your generous gifts," she said, waving at what they assumed were paintings propped against the wall.

"Under the circumstances, it is the least I could do. I have brought five paintings with me today," he said. When his gaze locked with Sarah's, Prue heard his sudden intake of breath.

Excellent. What man could resist such a stunning

creature? So why did she feel a tiny sliver of jealousy? Why did her stomach perform an odd flip?

Sarah smiled. "We heard the commotion, Prue, but did not want to add to your troubles."

Prue shrugged. "Everything is fine now."

Lord Roxbury turned to her, and her cheeks grew warm again. "Shall we be on our way?"

Sarah touched her on the arm. "You'd best hurry before Grandpapa thinks you are being kidnapped by the enemy."

Prue laughed, and she heard Lord Roxbury suck in another breath. She could hardly blame him. Most gentlemen gaped in awe of her sister's beguiling countenance. "Will you be all right here on your own until supper?"

"Of course." Sarah nodded. "Should there be an invasion, I hear Captain Lawrence is but a few miles away."

∽

The chilly breeze in the air caused Prue to shiver. She pulled her cape firmly around her shoulders as she settled into the leather carriage seat.

"You're certain you don't want to fetch a bonnet?" Lord Roxbury said, sitting opposite her.

In the close confines of the carriage, she felt oddly nervous. "No. I prefer to use the hood if I'm cold when walking outdoors. There is something quite liberating about feeling the wind tugging at your hair." Her declaration would make Sarah appear more refined.

Prue considered his impeccable attire. She supposed when one went about in society they had no choice but to follow ridiculous fashions. Indeed, with his neck buried beneath his shirt collars, she wondered if he was slowly suffocating.

His gaze travelled over her hair fastened loosely at her nape, and a faint smile touched his lips. "You're not one for convention, are you, Miss Pickle?"

Prue did not object to him calling her by that name. In truth, she found it endearing. "I struggle to see how an established set of rules should apply to an entirely different generation," she said, deciding it was better to be herself than to agree with him. And she had nothing to prove. Besides, compared to her, Sarah would appear all that a wife should be: affable, considerate, loving and good-natured. The sort of wife every lord wants.

Lord Roxbury sat forward. "But without a set of guiding principles, there would be anarchy, disorder."

"Yet such rigidity must surely stifle progression."

He smiled. "Those who break away from conformity often admit to their mistake."

"But what is a mistake if not a chance to learn?" she retorted.

He sat back in his seat and folded his arms across his chest. "Would it surprise you to learn that I have never been in the company of a lady who has challenged my point of view?"

"Yes," she said, raising a brow. "It would surprise me a great deal. It means you have spent your time in the company of pea-brained fools."

Lord Roxbury laughed.

She liked seeing the corners of his eyes crinkle. He looked handsome when he smiled, and the amber flecks in his hazel eyes were more prominent.

"Making your acquaintance has made that fact abundantly clear." He placed his top hat on the seat next to him and ran his fingers through brown hair a shade darker than her own.

Prue smiled. "I shall take that as a compliment."

"Please do."

Thinking of a way to fill the moment of awkward silence, Prue said, "Do you have something specific in mind for today?"

"I do."

"Is it to be a surprise?"

He laughed again. "No, Miss Pickle. We will take a tour of the house and the grounds. And I need advice about the plants in the orangery."

"Well, that shouldn't take too long. Perhaps if we finish early, you might come to the cottage. I am sure my sister would love to hear all about your plans to introduce her into society. She really is splendid company."

"I'm sure she is. But you can relay any information. I expect you will want to accompany her to Hagley Manor on Monday."

"Monday?" Prue shook her head as she remembered that was when he said the modiste was coming. Indeed, he must have paid her handsomely to attend at such short notice. "Oh, yes. It would not do to leave my sister alone in the company of an unmarried gentleman."

His eyes drifted languidly over her as though he had the ability to see through clothes. "You're alone with me. Do you not fear for your own reputation?"

Prue swallowed. "It … it is not the same," she said, despite her stomach performing an array of daring somersaults. "Men behave differently when in the company of beautiful women. I have no need to worry on that score."

He moistened his lips. "I think the definition of beauty is questionable. What appeals to one man repels another."

Prue gave an unladylike snort. "But a man would have to be blind not to consider Sarah beautiful. She will be an instant success. I am certain of it."

"I'm sure she will. No doubt there will be plenty of

eligible gentlemen lining up for an introduction and a place on her dance card."

Noting his distinct lack of enthusiasm, she said, "But not you?"

"No. Not me."

Prue would have to do something to change his mind. When he saw Sarah wearing a silk gown, when he saw tendrils of golden hair dangling seductively around her shoulders, he would think differently.

CHAPTER 4

The carriage rattled up the gravel drive and stopped in the middle of the cobblestone courtyard. Max jumped down and offered his hand to Miss Roxbury, noting the slight tremor in her fingers. Her touch sent a frisson of awareness shooting through him, a strange feeling of familiarity, a sense of rightness he had never experienced.

Bloody hell!

The pressure of finding a bride in the few months remaining caused all manner of strange thoughts to fill his head. It was unrealistic to expect he would marry for love, despite promising himself he would accept nothing less.

He could marry Miss Pickle.

He enjoyed her company, was curious to see if her passionate, unconventional nature would make her an immensely satisfying bed partner. Once the first few sparks of desire took hold, it would not take much to fan them into a raging inferno.

Damn. His cock twitched at the thought.

What a pity she seemed adamant to thrust him into the path of her sister.

"While we're here," he said, nodding to the stables to focus his mind, "perhaps we should ride out first. There's a chance of rain later, and I would not want you to catch a chill on my account. You do ride?"

"I do, but it's been two years since I was last in the saddle." She waved her hand down her simple brown dress. "I am hardly dressed for the occasion."

How stupid of him. Ladies were so confoundedly complicated when it came to choosing appropriate attire. "It is my fault. I should have mentioned my plans before we left your cottage. I should have at least given you a chance to change."

"It would not have made any difference." She shrugged and shook her head. "I no longer own a riding habit as I no longer own a horse."

Her words held no malice, yet he felt a stab of guilt when he considered all she had lost. "I see. Well, we will just have to take a tour of the house."

"I can go riding in this old thing." She tugged at the faded skirt. "I'll be warm enough with my cape, and these boots are sturdy."

Max glanced at the brown boots as she raised the hem of her dress. His gaze drifted a little higher as he imagined a slender calf and soft thigh, and he found he appreciated the considerate gesture. "I could not ask you to do that."

"You didn't ask. I offered. And it will be good to ride again." She marched past him and strode off toward the stables. She glanced back over her shoulder and shouted, "Are you coming?"

Once seated on their horses, they rode around the perimeter of the estate. Miss Roxbury pointed out various hills dotted along the horizon, naming them, explaining which one had the highest peak. She regaled tales of myth and folklore. Max doubted he had ever experienced a more fulfilling afternoon.

"There used to be a Saxon fort upon Briers Hill," she said as the wind whipped tendrils of brown hair loose. "Some claim to have seen the ghost of Edric standing on a crag waving his hammer and hollering a war cry."

Max snorted. "While such stories are entertaining, they're often started by the local drunkard."

"I'm inclined to agree with you," she said, leaning forward to pat the chestnut mare. "Have you been to the tower? I used to play there for hours as a girl until the walls started crumbling away and my parents deemed it unsafe."

"No. I've not had a chance to explore the local area."

She smirked. "It's on your land, in the wood behind the manor. I'll race you there."

Without another word, she charged across the field towards a group of trees in the distance. It wasn't difficult to catch up with her. Riding sidesaddle made her task all the more difficult. But he hung back a little, eager to watch her face alight with amusement, to see the faint sheen of exhilaration touch her cheeks. When she laughed and tried to beat him, the muscles in his abdomen grew hard and tight as he imagined rolling on top of her in the meadow, imagined plundering her sweet mouth until she gasped his name.

Bloody hell.

Never in his life had he wanted to bed a woman so badly. Miss Prudence Roxbury teased his mind and his cock. He found her witty, mysterious, and honest.

She was a rare find indeed.

"Oh, it's so wonderful to ride again after such a long time." The smile lighting up her face was a magnificent sight to behold.

Max practically jumped from his horse. His groom had

assisted her into the saddle, and now he had the splendid task of helping her down. She placed her hands on his shoulders, her fingers flexing around the muscles as she firmed her grip. Max knew his hands were shaking before clutching her waist, and when he eased her gently to the ground, he struggled to let go.

"My feet are firmly on the floor, my lord." She looked up at him and blinked.

"Excuse me?"

She frowned. "You can let go. I won't fall."

Max shook his head. "Forgive me. I thought you might be a little unsteady due to your lack of experience."

"Not at all." She raised her chin as he stepped away. "I used to ride daily before … well, before we moved to the cottage."

"You're welcome to come and ride here whenever it pleases you." The image of her straddling his naked body each night flashed into his mind.

She tilted her head to the side and stared into his eyes. "You know, I called you the most terrible things when I heard you'd come home to the manor. All of which I retract now, of course."

He inclined his head and grinned. "Of course."

"But I should like to know why you stayed away for so long. It's been nigh on two years since my father's death, and yet you've waited until now to claim what is rightfully yours."

Max supposed he owed her an explanation for evicting her from her home and then treating his inheritance with such blatant disregard.

"My father was obsessed with the thought of inheriting Hagley Manor. Apparently, our distant relatives were involved in a feud that divided the family. My father took great pleasure in the thought of possessing your family home."

"Oh, I see." She swallowed visibly and pursed her lips when he noticed them tremble. "But that still doesn't explain why you stayed away."

One would have to understand the nature of his father's spitefulness to understand Max's motive. "Even though my father is dead, I get an immense amount of pleasure knowing he would be disappointed."

She did not press him for a more detailed explanation. "Yet something made you change your mind."

He decided not to mention the stipulations of his father's will. As a consequence, Max had only inherited the entailed Roxbury Hall.

"I despised my father. I refuse to live at Roxbury Hall and have let the property to tenants. Despite inheriting this house from your father, I refused to entertain the thought of living at Hagley Manor. But without proper management, the house and lands will soon fall into disrepair. My father would have relished the prospect. Hence, my need to ensure it doesn't happen."

She stared at him, her eyes wide, her mouth open. "I-I did not mean to pry."

"You have a right to know the truth." He shrugged. "I know how you feel about the manor. Perhaps one day I will feel the same way about it, too."

They continued their walk through the woods in silence. Max wondered if the furrows on her brow stemmed from the neglect of her parents' beloved home.

The steep climb through the avenue of mature trees made her breathless. Max took her hand and placed it in the crook of his arm.

"So you intend to settle here." She clutched his arm as

they took the last few steps to the top. "You intend to make Hagley Manor your home."

The chance to start a new life was too tempting to resist. "I've grown tired of traipsing from one ball to another. It's a good six-hour ride from London, and here I can live as I please. Besides, in a few months I turn thirty and have an overwhelming desire to find something useful to do with my time."

"You mean to marry then?" she said with a level of eagerness he found a little unnerving.

"Of course."

"There are many suitable ladies living locally."

"Are there?" He glanced at her profile, at the way her lips formed a perfect pout when she was thinking. "I believe only one lady has attracted my attention."

Her head shot round, her curious gaze locking with his. They fell silent for a moment, and all he could hear were the birds chirping and the wind's whispers rustling in the trees.

With a blush, she turned away. "Sarah knows the house just as well as I do. Perhaps she could come and show you around. She has a far more eloquent manner and is always good company."

"You said it wouldn't do for your sister to be alone with me. So I suppose I shall just have to console myself with the thought of spending more time with you."

"Will it be such a hardship?"

The surrounding air sparked to life. A frisson of excitement coursed through his veins at the prospect of seeing her again. "It will be no hardship at all."

They stared at each other. He would have given anything to know her thoughts.

Thankfully they came to the top of the path. Max's heart was racing, but it had nothing to do with the exhausting climb. He spotted a wooden bridge built over a large pond.

The water looked murky green. Not even the faintest ripple was evident on the stagnant surface.

"Don't step close to the edge," she said, changing the subject. They walked across the narrow bridge that amounted to nothing more than a few flimsy planks. "I shall never forget the time I thought to paddle my feet. The water looks shallow, but the visible layer of silt is definitely not the bed."

"Am I to assume you soon realised your error?" He was smiling before she finished the story.

"I got stuck in the mud, right up to my neck. It took three people to pull me out. I can still hear the squelching noise as I struggled to walk home."

Max pursed his lips to suppress a chuckle. "When was this?"

"Last Friday."

He could feel his eyes bulging from their sockets as he repeated, "Last Friday!"

"I'm only teasing. It was years ago." Then the corners of her mouth twitched, and her eyes sparkled before she burst into uncontrollable fits of laughter.

The sound was infectious, and he laughed until his ribs ached.

"I ... I assume that's the tower you mentioned?" he said, catching his breath before nodding to the dilapidated stone structure behind her.

The door was missing. A flight of steps led to the woodland canopy now acting as the roof. At one time, it must have been a lookout post. Now, the encroaching vegetation clung to the walls as if helping to keep it upright.

"It is." She looked at the building with an air of wonder. "If we're careful we can step inside."

Max glanced at the array of odd-shaped stones on the ground.

In her excitement, and perhaps sensing his hesitation, she grabbed his hand. "Come. We'll stay but a minute."

Suddenly, in his mind, it was no longer a place to spy on potential invaders or an old ruin hiding away in the woods. It was a place for lovers to indulge in secret fantasies. It was a place where one's deepest desires knew no limits or restrictions.

Lust clawed away inside. As she pulled him over the threshold, he knew he should resist. He knew he would struggle to keep it at bay.

It felt much smaller inside the circular stone building than he imagined. The confined space made him more aware of how close she stood. The private nature of their conversation had created a level of intimacy he had not shared with a woman before. He found himself possessed by the thought that everything would be different with her.

"A violent storm destroyed the rotten timbers long before my father lived here." She stared up at a sky of puffy grey clouds obscured somewhat by thick branches. "If money were no object, I would love to restore it. I've often wondered what it would be like to sleep in a tower."

Sleep would not be the activity he had in mind.

She was still holding his hand, and he could feel the pulse of desire travel down his arm to beat against her palm. When he failed to comment, she turned to face him, and his gaze fell to her mouth. The air grew warm, the apples of her cheeks flaming as he stepped closer.

"Tell me." His words were but a whisper as he brushed his knee against her dress. "Tell me again why you feel safe with me, why you believe yourself impervious to seduction?"

She swallowed in response to his languid tone. "Well, is ... isn't it obvious?"

"Not to me."

Her nervous gaze drifted over his face. "Because I ... I do not possess the physical attributes gentlemen find pleasing."

"I must disagree." He bowed his head until the brim of his top hat touched her hair. The need to taste her overwhelmed him. "Everything about you pleases me. From the deep pink hue of your lips to the gentle curve of your hips. I enjoy seeing you smile. I like the way your eyes light up the room when you're amused. I find your honesty highly arousing and—"

"Heavens!" She put her hand on her chest. "Are you determined to make me swoon?"

He wanted to sate his curiosity. He wanted to discover the depth of the passionate nature he knew brimmed beneath the surface. Bloody hell. He had never felt so consumed with the need to join with a woman.

"You know you want to hear all the things I've been keeping to myself for days." His mouth was but an inch from her temple. "I've not stopped thinking about you. I've not stopped wondering—"

"No," she cried. "You mustn't think, and you mustn't wonder."

"I know you want me to kiss you."

She looked up at him. He recognised the glazed look of desire and when she opened her mouth to protest he covered it with his own.

God damn, she tasted so sweet.

Max had not expected an immediate response and was surprised when a soft moan escaped from her lips. The sound spurred him on to progress from the chaste melding of mouths, and he dared to let his tongue trace the smooth seam. He felt a shift in her as soon as he penetrated her mouth. With a sudden burst of enthusiasm, she grabbed the lapels of his coat, pressed her body into his and deepened the kiss.

Their actions became fraught with unfulfilled desire. He pushed her back against the crumbling wall as his tongue delved deeper to tangle and dance with hers. She knocked off his hat, her hands running wildly through his hair. His hands travelled down her back to cup her plump cheeks as he pressed his aching cock against her stomach.

Good Lord.

It took all the strength he had not to bunch her dress up to her waist and thrust home. Catrina liked it rough and hard and the sobering thought caused him to break contact. It was wrong of him to treat Prudence with the same lack of respect.

"Forgive me," he said between breathless pants as he tore his lips away. He was aware of the rapid rise and fall of her chest, and he fought the urge to claim her mouth again. "I don't know what came over me."

She stared at him. Shock marred her brow. "I ... I don't know what to say. I never expected ... well, I would expect such a thing to happen to Sarah."

Why did everything come back to her sister?

Could the lady not see she had an inherent appeal of her own?

"Let us put it down to excitement, upon discovering the tower," he suggested, though he knew he would find an opportunity to kiss her again, and soon. He picked up his hat and dusted it off. "Let's step outside, pretend this place is a gateway to another realm. One where the bonds of constraint no longer apply."

She gazed up at the unusual structure. "I used to pretend it was a magical place. How strange that you would consider it to be the same."

Guilt flared. He didn't consider it to be the same at all. It was a case of placating her, a way to ease her conscience.

"Precisely. Once we leave here, things will be exactly as they were before."

She smiled and nodded. "Then lead the way."

Nothing would be the same. Fate had conspired to bring him to Hagley Manor. Lust conspired to provide the answer to his prayers.

He was going to marry Prudence Pickle.

He was going to claim his inheritance, stamp all over his father's grave and give a loud chuckle. It didn't matter that she didn't love him. Indeed, love played no part in his decision. She loved Hagley Manor, and that would be enough. The marriage would unite the two families. It would help to heal the wounds of the past. And his father would have many sleepless nights in Hell knowing there was not a damn thing he could do about it.

CHAPTER 5

THE REST OF THE DAY PASSED QUICKLY.

Prue gave Lord Roxbury a tour of the house. They discussed the servants, put names to all the solemn faces in gilt frames gracing the walls of the picture gallery. Conversation flowed. They laughed at the strange-looking plants in the orangery. She ran away from him while showing him the way through the maze. Then she sat on the grass and waited for twenty minutes until he found the exit.

All the time, she pretended she was fulfilling her part of the agreement to act as a guide in return for Sarah's new dresses. All the time, she pretended they had never ventured into the magical tower. But the feeling of his warm mouth moving on hers would be forever ingrained in her memory. Whenever he spoke or smiled, her gaze drifted to his full lips. Whenever she caught sight of his tongue, a sudden heat flamed in her chest.

When she lay in her bed that night, she chastised herself for being so fickle, for succumbing so easily, for being seduced by a few flattering words and a wolfish grin. The same questions bounced back and forth in her mind. What possible reason could he have had for kissing her?

Would he attempt to do so again?

Perhaps he pitied her. After all, he had inherited their home and left them squashed into the tiny cottage with barely room to breathe. Yes, that must surely be the reason behind his kind words and amorous overtures.

When she closed her eyes, the smell of leather, shaving soap and the mysterious ingredient that had the power to numb all inhibitions flooded her senses. The strange yearning returned. The odd feeling that made her body crave unfamiliar things, that made the womanly place between her thighs throb at the thought of his touch.

God help her! She wanted him!

At four-and-twenty, she'd thought it too late to think about affairs of the heart. Although in Lord Roxbury's case, it did not seem to be a problem for her traitorous mind and body.

The whole thing was utterly ridiculous. Lord Roxbury was to marry Sarah. The thought caused guilt to flare. An image of her sister's sweet face flashed into her mind, only to fizzle out and be replaced by the vision of a naked lord with a muscular chest and a wicked mouth in need of claiming.

It took her another hour to get to sleep, and she was forced to open a window to cool her heated blood. But as the days passed, the memory faded into the far recesses of her mind, lost amongst all the other doubts and fears she refused to give a voice.

When the day came for them to visit Hagley Manor, to meet the modiste and receive dance tuition from Monsieur Lalonde, Prue made it her mission to ensure Lord Roxbury fell in love with Sarah.

How difficult could it be?

The gentleman had a weakness for kissing, and once he

took the time to notice Sarah's perfect pout, he would be desperate to take her to the tower and indulge his whims.

Prue's chest grew tight at the thought, and she sucked in a breath to banish it.

"I say, don't you think it's rather rude?" Grandpapa said as they all sat in Lord Roxbury's carriage. "One of us should have stayed at home to greet Captain Lawrence and his men."

"The captain asked his friend, Lord Roxbury, to entertain us while he made a thorough search of the area." Prue hated lying to her grandfather, but she couldn't leave him on his own for fear he might scare one of their neighbours. Her heart ached when she recalled how strong-minded and independent he used to be. Many times he was like his old self, and she was sure these forgetful episodes would pass.

"Ah, well, at least we'll be able to rest easier in our beds tonight," he said as he narrowed his gaze and scoured the passing fields.

Sarah tapped her on the arm. "I don't know about resting easier. I must admit to feeling a little nervous about today."

"Why? I'm sure it will all be very pleasant. The girls will love roaming the estate again, and Henry has promised to keep Grandpapa company." All in all, Lord Roxbury had been extremely accommodating. "I can't wait to see what fabrics the modiste has in mind for you."

"Perhaps it is just nerves," Sarah said. "Despite having had dance lessons in the past, Monsieur Lalonde sounds rather exotic."

"Shush." Prue tapped her finger to her lips. Her frantic gaze flew to the seat opposite, and she was grateful their grandfather suffered from poor hearing. "You mean, Mr Smith, the dance tutor Lord Roxbury sent for from Bath."

Sarah sighed wearily. "Sorry, Prue, I forgot. I can see it being rather an eventful day."

Prue pushed aside her fears, suppressed the strange

tickling feeling in her stomach at the thought of seeing Lord Roxbury again. "Everything will work out perfectly. I am sure of it."

∼

Max heard the rumble of carriage wheels coming up the drive and strode out to greet his guests. He had spent the last few days visiting tenants, inspecting ledgers, anticipating Prudence Roxbury's reaction when their eyes met again.

As if the kiss in the tower wasn't enough to convince him of their compatibility, the afternoon spent bantering and laughing confirmed his decision. She made him feel at ease, relaxed — although he had feared he would never find his way out of that blasted maze. Conversation flowed naturally. He respected her opinion which to his mind provided the solid foundation necessary for a successful marriage. Indeed, he would be a better man than his father: he would enjoy spending time in his wife's company.

The carriage crunched on the gravel as it slowed to a halt. Henry jumped down from his perch, opened the door and lowered the steps. In a matter of seconds, the tranquil surroundings became a hive of activity. The children's excited chatter filled the air, the wide beams on their faces revealing their obvious pleasure at seeing their family home again.

Prudence's grandfather introduced himself as Mr Hargrove. "Very good of you to assist Captain Lawrence in his duties," he said, coming to stand in front of Max and patting him on the upper arm. He glanced up at the cloudless sky. "I have promised the girls a game of bowls. There used to be a set around here somewhere. But for the life of me, I cannot remember when I last played."

Max put his hand on the old man's shoulder. He looked

tired and weary. "I'm sure Henry will find it, and he even has my permission to play."

Henry cast him a wide smile as he helped Sarah Roxbury from the carriage.

Wearing a deep blue spencer that enhanced her eyes to perfection, the lady was a stunning beauty. Max was confident she would soon secure a husband within their ranks. Indeed, Sarah Roxbury was the epitome of summer: bright and radiant.

She offered a curtsy and smiled, and he could not help but admire God's creation.

But there was nothing surprising about summer. Nothing to stimulate the mind, nothing beneath what the eye could see.

Then Prudence descended, and the muscles in his abdomen grew tight as the urge to bed the woman who'd be his wife took hold. In contrast, Prudence Roxbury was like spring. There was always something new to see, something mysterious and magical happening beneath the surface.

"Miss Roxbury." Max inclined his head as his eyes devoured her.

She blushed, and he suppressed a triumphant grin. When she moistened her lips, Max knew her mind was engaged in remembering the kiss in the tower.

Excellent.

If he fanned the flame of desire, she would be his before the week was out.

"My lord," she said. "Thank you for welcoming us all to your home." She sounded composed, confident. Yet her countenance faltered when her gaze slipped to his lips.

Max smiled. "Shall we go and meet—"

"You can tell us all about it once we're inside." Prudence rushed to his side. Before he could say another word, she tugged his arm. "Grandpapa is desperate to explore and need not hear about our plans." She bent her head and whispered, "I assume Monsieur Lalonde and Madame Duval are French. It would not be wise to mention it to my grandfather. Not while he is still a little confused. He will assume they are spies come to snoop on Captain Lawrence."

"Forgive me," Max said, inhaling the sweet smell of apples that clung to her hair. "It had not occurred to me that it would be a problem." He glanced back over his shoulder to see Henry scurrying off with her relatives. "They will soon be too occupied with their game to worry about what's going on in the house."

"It's not your fault." She let go of his arm as they walked up the steps and into the hall. "It's something we are used to dealing with."

"I can ease your fears somewhat. While Monsieur Lalonde is a rather extravagant Frenchman, Madame Duval is from Cheapside. However, she speaks with a feigned French burr."

"Cheapside?" She wrinkled her nose.

"One can charge an inflated price for their work if their clients believe they trained in Paris."

Prudence's eyes twinkled. "How interesting. I can't wait to meet her."

"As to that." Max shuffled uncomfortably. "Madame Duval has commanded a bedchamber. She insists on using the room with the best natural light." He inclined his head. "I'm to accompany you upstairs to make the necessary introductions. I trust that will not pose a problem."

"Only should you wish to remain there," Prudence said.

He had no desire to watch Sarah Roxbury undress. However, Miss Pickle was another matter. To glimpse her soft thighs would be worth the price of fifty dresses.

Max escorted them upstairs, only to discover that the room had been Prudence's old bedchamber.

"It is exactly the same as the day I left," she said, rushing to the window that offered a perfect view of the gardens. She turned and gazed at the four-poster bed. "May I?" she asked with an air of excitement.

The mischievous glint in her eye held him spellbound. "Of course," he said, yet had not the slightest idea of her intention.

Removing her cape and draping it over the chair, she climbed onto the large bed.

"It must be three times the size of the bed you have at the cottage," Sarah said.

"Oh, what I would give to stretch my legs out without my toes peeking out of the bottom." She lay back on the mound of pillows and opened her arms wide. "See my fingers don't even touch the edges."

In his mind, she lay sprawled across the coverlet as naked as the day she was born. In his mind, she beckoned him over with her finger, the wicked look in her eye telling him all he needed to know.

Max shook his head and cleared his throat. Any more erotic musings and he'd not be decent company in such tight breeches.

A light tap on the door captured their attention. Prudence jumped down from the bed and straightened her dress.

"Ah, my lord. I'm told the ladies are 'ere." Madame Duval hovered at the door.

Max suppressed a snigger as he stepped aside. "Please come in, Madame Duval." The woman sounded more Scottish than French. Thankfully, her skill for design far outweighed her acting ability.

Her large bosom entered the room first while the rest of her followed behind. The modiste was small in stature with a narrow waist that proved to be thoroughly out of proportion with the rest of her body. In the daylight, her complexion had a faint purple hue which he attributed to her tight stays.

Madame Duval stepped forward and took hold of Sarah's hands. "Am I to have the pleasure of dressing this delightful creature?"

"You are."

Panic flared. She would dress them both, but he had not yet told Prudence of his plans.

"Are you certain this room is to your liking?" Max asked to distract the modiste.

"Oh, *oui*. It is perfect," Madame Duval said with a smirk. She had dressed Catrina on a number of occasions, and he placed his faith in her discretion. "Please wait out in the hall while I measure the lady. I have brought a few samples with me which can be adjusted at short notice."

"We shall leave her in your capable hands."

Max hadn't mentioned that Sarah's introduction into society would take place eleven days, hence. He had invited a few friends and acquaintances from London to stay for the weekend. An informal country gathering would help to ease her in gently. Of course, he hoped at least one gentleman would be dazzled by Sarah Roxbury's stunning beauty.

"We will wait outside," Prue said, patting down a few stray locks. "Call me if you need me."

They left Sarah admiring fabrics with Madame Duval. Max closed the chamber door behind him. Picking up a chair from farther along the hallway, he placed it next to Prudence's chair and sat down with her to wait.

"I know I seem eager for Sarah to have a come out," Prudence said, "but I wouldn't wish to put Madame Duval under any pressure."

Max was going to wait until later to broach the subject of the party. "I told Madame Duval we need at least two dresses ready for next weekend. I am having a gathering here. A rather select house party where your sister will gain the opportunity to meet some people. Call it an informal introduction into society. That way, when she makes her debut in London, she will feel more at ease. No doubt her beauty will be the talk of the *ton* and will encourage only the best offers."

Prudence narrowed her gaze. "I know I said things are more relaxed in the country, but Sarah cannot stay here on her own. Who will act as her chaperone?"

"You will." He offered her a reassuring smile. "And your grandfather and sisters will be here, of course."

All the colour drained from her face, and when she opened her mouth to speak her bottom lip quivered. "But Grandpapa cannot spend time with strangers. He can be unstable. It will make him nervous."

"Henry will take care of your grandfather. He can keep to his room, mostly."

"But you don't understand. People will mock him. They will be unkind."

"Then I will send them tumbling down the front steps with my boot attached to their behind."

"Why do you make everything sound so simple when you know it will not be the case?"

Max noted the genuine look of fear in her eyes and his heart went out to her. "Then I shall ask my Aunt Gwendoline to come and act as chaperone." She had always been fond of him, and when he told her of his plans to marry, she would be ecstatic. "We will say your grandfather is ill in bed, and Henry will keep him company, as will your sisters."

She was silent for a moment. "You want us all to stay here?" Her gaze fell to his lips, and he suppressed a confident grin.

"No one knows the house and staff better than you. I will need your help if Sarah is to be a success."

"Perhaps when you see her wearing a pretty dress, you might change your mind about filling a place on her dance card."

"Perhaps," he said purely to placate her. "And you might save a place for me on your card, too."

She ignored his comment, shook her head and frowned. "But I haven't a thing to wear that would be suitable. I fear I would only ruin Sarah's chances of making a good match."

Max sat back in the chair and folded his arms across his chest. "Which is why I have asked Madame Duval to measure you for new dresses, too." Indeed, he had given the modiste a few instructions regarding the design.

"New dresses," she gasped. "I can't let you do that."

Max suppressed a grin. "As the eldest, you must set an example. People will judge you just as much as your sister." He would not have his betrothed mistaken for the hired help.

"Well." The word came out as more of a sigh. "I shall contribute towards the cost. It was never part of our agreement for you to provide me with fripperies."

"We agreed that I would introduce your sister and so your dresses are a necessary part of our arrangement."

Silence ensued.

"I suppose you're right." She gave a funny wave. "But I will find a way to repay you for your kindness."

His gaze travelled over her, noting that her breasts were just the right size to fit nicely into his palm. "Oh, I'm sure I will think of something you can do."

CHAPTER 6

Hagley Manor hummed with activity as the staff rushed about making the final preparations for the guests due to arrive within the hour.

Prue smoothed her hands down the pale pink dress and then fiddled with the burgundy ribbon that enhanced the fitted bodice. Madame Duval insisted the style suited her figure to perfection yet if she bent her head, her chin almost touched her expanding bosom. Indeed, when Lord Roxbury first saw her, he struggled to make eye contact.

"Madame Duval has done an exquisite job," he said as he met her in the hall. His gaze fell to the scooped neckline and lingered there for longer than deemed appropriate. As he moistened his lips, the sight of his tongue caused an odd little flip in her stomach.

"Wait until you see Sarah," she said, trying to banish the strange fluttering sensation. The week spent helping him to organise the house in readiness for the weekend's activities had fed her secret craving for him. "The sky-blue muslin is breathtaking."

"Yes," he said, stifling a yawn. "I met her and Aunt

Gwendoline a few minutes ago on the landing. They'll be down momentarily."

"Your aunt seems pleased to be playing hostess this weekend."

His aunt was a robust woman with a warm, pleasant demeanour. The matron's jolly countenance had put Prue at ease immediately. There were no feigned airs and graces. Prue suppressed a chuckle when she recalled the way the lady had ruffled Lord Roxbury's hair by way of a greeting, as if he were still a boy of ten.

"She enjoys matchmaking almost as much as she enjoys gossiping," he replied. "Both my aunt and my mother married young to avoid the pitfalls of entailment, and so she understands your plight more than most."

Was that why Gwendoline was so friendly and accommodating?

Prue glanced up at the oak staircase, her mind lost in happy memories of the past. "It feels rather strange being back here again. I can't recall the last time I heard music and laughter filling the rooms."

He offered a sympathetic smile. "I'm certain your parents would approve. Your efforts to ensure your sister makes an excellent match are commendable."

"And I am sure they would approve of you, my lord. You have excelled in your commitment to our cause." And he could have saved himself the trouble of hosting a social event if only he'd stopped and taken more notice of Sarah.

Lord Roxbury inhaled deeply at the obvious compliment before his gaze fell once more to the neckline of her dress. "It appears I may have excelled on two counts."

Her cheeks flamed at his salacious comment. Struggling to form a response, she said, "How many people are coming?"

While his lips curved up into a sinful grin, his eyes sparkled with amusement. "There are eight, Miss Pickle."

"Don't call me that in front of the guests," she whispered as she glanced nervously over her shoulder.

"There's no one here," he chuckled. "But rest assured. I shall only refer to it when we're alone, which I expect to be quite often. It will be my pet name for you. I shall—"

"Pet name?" she scrunched up her nose. "I'm not a dog. Don't expect me to roll over so you can tickle my stomach."

"I wouldn't dream of doing such a thing unless you wanted me to. I'd happily settle for a playful nip and to hear you panting."

Prue gasped.

"Forgive me," he said with a smirk, "did I say that aloud?"

What was wrong with him? He had the same wild look as the day he'd kissed her in the tower. Too much country air was known to affect the mind. It made one less inhibited, but in Lord Roxbury's case, he had taken on the manner of a skilled seducer.

"You mentioned there were a few eligible gentlemen in the party." Prue decided to tease him. Being made to feel like a naive girl was beginning to grate. "Perhaps I might partake in a little flirtatious banter. After all, there may be a man amongst them to make me change my mind about marriage."

His expression darkened. "You won't like any of them. You are far too smart and witty to be lumbered with a dunce or dolt."

Prue's eyes widened, and she suppressed a blush at the compliment. "I cannot see Sarah wanting to spend a lifetime with such a gentleman, either. I think she needs a man who is charitable, has an interest in philosophy. One who is strong enough to stand by his principles."

And adventurous enough to indulge in amorous kisses in a tower, she added silently. Sarah needed a gentleman like Lord Roxbury.

WHAT EVERY LORD WANTS

Lord Roxbury moistened his lips. "And what do *you* need, Miss Pickle?"

Prue stared at his mouth while she contemplated the question. Her mind was suddenly filled with thoughts of his lustful pants and groans. She swallowed down her nerves, deciding honesty was the best policy.

"I need someone to laugh with when the days are grey and cloudy, when the world tilts on its axis to throw us off kilter. I need someone who is honest, considerate, who would love me and no other."

Lord Roxbury's gaze searched her face. "You made no mention of passion or desire. No mention of physical attributes."

Prue shrugged. She wanted a man who made her heart flutter as Lord Roxbury did but she was hardly in a position to say that. "I would like the gentleman to have fiery red hair and a beard long enough to touch his chest. I would like him to wear a kilt so that I might stare at his strong, sturdy legs all day long."

A smile touched the corners of his mouth. "I should not have asked, as now I feel so hopelessly inadequate."

"Oh, you're more than adequate, my lord." Prue paused for effect. "Sarah has never been as fussy as I am."

"Good. As I have invited a few gentlemen who are of a mind to wed. And a few others to even up the numbers."

Prue smiled to suppress her sudden flurry of nerves. Having helped him with the sleeping arrangements and allocating the rooms, she recalled there were a few ladies on the list, too. "I shall never remember all of their names."

He turned to face her fully, his gaze roaming over her hair, lingering on her lips. "You've nothing to fear. All will be well. I crossed the ogres off the list and replaced them with dullards. After a few glasses of port, most of them don't know their own names, either."

Heavens. By the sound of it, Sarah's prospects of making a match were diminishing by the second.

The sound of carriage wheels crunching on the gravel drive captured their attention.

"It would appear our first guest has arrived," Lord Roxbury said with an eager smile.

"I shall run and fetch your aunt." Prue didn't give him a chance to object and dashed up the stairs in search of the matron.

Prue spent the next few hours hovering in the hall with Sarah, watching Lord Roxbury and his aunt greet their guests. After the introductions were made, they agreed to assist Aunt Gwendoline in giving a tour of the house.

His aunt had claimed Sarah as her partner, leaving Prue with Lord Roxbury. They had the pleasure of showing Mr Lucas Dempsey and his wife, Helena, to their room.

"Anthony assures me he is coming," Mr Dempsey said. His wife held on to his arm as they mounted the stairs. "It is not like him to be late."

"Well, I did not give him much notice." Lord Roxbury shrugged. "Perhaps he's delayed with estate business." He turned to Prue as they stopped on the landing. "Didn't we allocate the Dempsey's the blue room?"

Prue gave a frustrated sigh. He really was extremely forgetful. "No," she said, rolling her eyes at Mrs Dempsey who chuckled in response. "We said the room with the best view of the garden." She turned to the guests. "Lord Roxbury told me of your recent renovations to your own garden, and I thought you would appreciate what has been done here. Of course, it has been neglected a little of late, but Lord Roxbury intends to rectify the situation."

Mrs Dempsey smiled. "How thoughtful of you." She glanced at her husband. "We do so love spending time outdoors."

The corners of Mr Dempsey's mouth curled up into a smile. "Indeed, we have spent many happy hours frolicking in the garden."

"Well, you are most welcome to frolic in this one. It has been years since anyone has taken the time to appreciate the flora and fauna."

Mr Dempsey inclined his head. He really was an extremely handsome gentleman. "I am certain we will be gasping with pleasure in such fetching surroundings."

"There is an excellent statue of the Roman goddess Venus."

"A statue," Mrs Dempsey repeated softly as her cheeks flushed. "It sounds as though your garden caters to all our needs."

A sense of pride filled Prue's chest.

She glanced at Lord Roxbury, who was staring intently at her.

"What would I do without you, Miss Roxbury?" His tone sounded silky smooth, and the air about them whirled with a suppressed sensuality that made her feel as though her body was swaying to and fro.

Prue blinked to bring her mind back to the present. "You would get yourself into a complete muddle, my lord." She almost forgot other people were witnessing their exchange.

"Then I shall have to lock you up in a chamber and keep you here indefinitely."

Prue snorted. "With that flamboyant knot in your cravat, you hardly rouse an image of a gothic villain."

Lord Roxbury raised a brow as his gaze raked over her. "Oh, I can be quite determined when I have a mind to be." His compelling gaze held her riveted to the spot. He glanced at Mr Dempsey and inclined his head. "Forgive us. When it comes to banter, we tend to get a little over eager in our bid to outdo the other."

"Please, do not apologise on our account." Mr Dempsey gave an indolent wave. "I have never been one to follow convention. I much prefer to be in the company of like-minded people. Indeed, your witty exchange has left me entertained and invigorated."

"Well, they say a good host should anticipate his guests' needs," Lord Roxbury said. "No doubt we will continue to entertain you during your stay."

Prue sighed. "He takes great pleasure in teasing me as I'm sure you've noticed."

Mrs Dempsey smiled. "You know, a stroll in the garden can work to calm a volatile spirit. Perhaps you should both take a turn outdoors, let the fresh breeze soothe the soul."

The comment brought to mind their last spell outdoors, the one that led to the most sinful kiss of her entire life.

Lord Roxbury gestured to the long corridor. "Let us show you to your room and then we will consider your suggestion." As the couple walked on ahead, he turned to Prue and whispered, "Perhaps we should venture to the tower. I've heard the view can rouse a deep stirring in the chest. I've heard it can be quite a satisfying experience that should be—"

"Shush." She did not need reminding of his warm lips and muscular thighs.

Mrs Dempsey glanced over her shoulder and smiled. "I assume our room is on the right?"

Prue rushed forward. "Yes, it's this room." She opened the door and stood back for them to enter.

Mr Dempsey strode over to the window. "You're right. The view is splendid. And if I'm not mistaken, you have a willow tree."

"Yes." As a child, Prue had spent many hours playing under the hanging branches. "You could hide for hours beneath the branches, and no one would ever find you."

He glanced at his wife. "Interesting."

"I'm afraid I'm still not used to country hours," Lord Roxbury began, "but have been forced to compromise and so we shall dine at seven. In the meantime, you are welcome to rest or stroll around the garden. Refreshments will be served all day in the drawing room. Should you wish to ride, you will find Bagshaw in the stables, and he will happily assist you."

Mr Dempsey turned to face them. "Thank you, Max. Will you alert me the moment Anthony arrives?"

"Certainly."

Mrs Dempsey followed them to the door and closed it gently behind them.

"They think we are far too familiar," Prue said, marching along the corridor as Lord Roxbury followed her. "I saw the look in her eye when she suggested we stroll outdoors. They believe we are conducting a liaison."

"Well, there is a grain of truth to it," he replied. "Our amorous tryst in the tower would be considered enough to secure a betrothal had anyone witnessed the event."

She stopped and thrust her hands on her hips. "It was not a tryst."

"What was it then?"

Prue exhaled loudly as she waved her hand in the air. "It was a silly moment of madness. A silly moment that will not be repeated."

Sinful eyes devoured her as he stepped forward, backing her into the wall. "I don't know why you deny your feelings," he said, his hot breath breezing over her neck. "I can only assume it has something to do with your sister. But you should know that I will never offer for a woman who does not ignite a fiery passion in my breast." His gaze dropped to her lips, and she realised she wanted him to kiss her. "You should know that my body aches and burns to kiss you again."

Prue stared at him as he scanned the scandalous neckline of her new dress. Good Lord. Her cheeks flamed, and she struggled to catch her breath. He pressed closer, his knee nudging the gap between her legs.

A noise to their left captured their attention, and Lord Roxbury stepped away just as his aunt mounted the top stair with Sarah and two other guests in tow.

"There you are, Roxbury." Aunt Gwendoline stopped to catch her breath. "I have been looking for you everywhere."

Lord Roxbury's expression darkened. Indeed, Prue had never seen him look so serious. What had his aunt done to cause such a dramatic change in his countenance?

"Lord Mannerly has arrived with Mrs Beecham." Aunt Gwendoline shook her head. "For the life of me, I can't remember which room she is in."

Lord Roxbury stood frozen to the spot, his stern gaze focusing on the recent arrivals.

"Is something amiss?" Prue whispered. She fought the urge to touch his arm, to offer comfort for whatever had roused his ire. Perhaps it had something to do with the fact he had neglected to mention Mrs Beecham would be attending. Prue had no recollection of her being on the guest list.

He shook his head and muttered, "No, nothing is amiss. It is simply that I do not wish to cause you any embarrassment with my over-familiarity."

It suddenly occurred to her that she enjoyed his attention despite her protests to the contrary. "No one saw us. If we've made a mistake with the rooms, the one at the end of the hall is empty."

"Be a darling," Aunt Gwendoline said, hovering near the

stairs, "and show Mrs Beecham to her room while we play escort to Lord Mannerly."

With his huge frame, Lord Mannerly towered over the ladies. His immaculate mop of golden hair and his foppish dress suggested a man overly concerned with appearances. Indeed, he was adept at capturing the ladies' attention as both Sarah and Gwendoline kept staring at his pleasing countenance and giggled like girls whenever he spoke.

Lord Roxbury clenched his jaw but conceded to his aunt's wishes.

"This way, Mrs Beecham."

Mrs Beecham walked towards them. Prue felt positively frumpy in comparison. The lady's cornflower-blue pelisse, trimmed with white rosettes to match the white ostrich feather in her over-sized straw hat, spoke of sophistication in character as well as experience.

"My lord." A secretive smile played at the corners of Mrs Beecham's mouth. "How good it is to see you again."

"Your room is a little further down the hall. I am sure you wish to rest and change after the long journey." Lord Roxbury's eyes held no emotion as he spoke. "Please follow me."

"Aren't you forgetting your manners, my lord?" Mrs Beecham glanced at Prue, her smirk causing the muscle in her cheek to twitch.

Lord Roxbury gave a curt nod. "Mrs Beecham, may I present Miss Prudence Roxbury."

They both curtsied.

"Welcome, Mrs Beecham. I hope you will enjoy your stay at Hagley Manor." Prue waved to the door beyond their shoulder. "Let me show you to your room."

"Please, you must call me Catrina. You're obviously family and Max is such a dear friend."

Lord Roxbury scowled as tension and animosity

emanated from him. "Thank you for your assistance, Miss Roxbury. You may go and seek refreshment while I show Mrs Beecham the way."

Prue searched his face. Never, during all the times she'd conversed with him, had she seen such an austere expression. His solemn mood had something to do with the new arrivals. Still, that did not mean he should be so cold to her. Indeed, the tight pain in her chest was slowly working its way up to her throat. She could not decide whether this strange emotion was brought about by pain or anger at his sudden indifference.

Struggling to form a reply, she simply inclined her head to them both and marched towards the stairs. As she reached the top, she turned to see Lord Roxbury follow Mrs Beecham into the room and close the door.

With the pain now restricting her airways, she made her way out into the garden. The fresh breeze drifted across her face, and she closed her eyes and inhaled.

Why had his mood affected her so deeply? Why did she care that he had accompanied the lady into her private chamber? Jealousy slithered through her, leaving a feeling of inadequacy in its wake. Her eyes flew open at the realisation that she had formed an attachment to the man who had kissed her with such unbridled passion. Since that moment, she had been fooling herself, pretending she could watch him marry her sister and be happy for them.

It was all a lie.

Prue wanted Lord Roxbury — as her friend, her lover, her husband.

She plastered her hand over her mouth as the thought infused her mind and body. Disappointment and the pain of loss had been her constant companions. Fear lingered, too. Could she ever be the sort of woman the lord would want?

Perhaps she should encourage his amorous overtures, gauge his response.

Guilt flared.

But Sarah had never shown any interest in Lord Roxbury. And she believed the house party genuinely was a means for her to become accustomed to mingling with society's elite.

With a renewed sense of determination, Prue sucked in a breath and straightened her shoulders. One way or another, she would have Lord Roxbury. She would have to be subtle, of course. Perhaps she could befriend Mrs Dempsey. It was obvious her husband worshipped her. Indeed, the lady had married the most handsome man in all of England.

How did one get a man to fall in love with them?

How did one become the sort of lady every lord wants?

CHAPTER 7

Max slammed the door to the bedchamber, barely able to control his raging temper. "What the bloody hell are you doing here?"

Catrina placed her hand over her heart. "Come now, is that any way to greet me after all we've been to each other?" She took a step closer, and Max backed away.

"What do you want, Catrina?" He clenched his jaw so hard he was in danger of cracking his teeth. "I doubt you've come to enjoy the country air."

She gave a coy smile. "I wanted to see you. Is that so terrible? Is it a crime?" She pulled the pins from her hat and placed them on the dresser.

"You're not staying." God, he would drag her away kicking and screaming if he had to. "My coachman will take you as far as the nearest inn. He will drive you all the way back to London if you agree to leave now."

Placing the straw monstrosity on the bed, she unbuttoned her pelisse. "I'm sure the last thing you want is to make a scene." Stepping towards him wearing a sultry smirk, she shrugged out of the garment and let it fall to the floor. "Let me stay, Max. Perhaps you might be a little cold tonight. Perhaps you might enjoy my company again."

Max considered the prospect for less than a second. They had used each other to suppress their boredom. Her constant demands grated, robbed the pleasure from every liaison. He believed her to be untrustworthy, eager to lie to gain favour. No. He had no desire to indulge her whims.

"Enjoy your company again?" he scoffed. "Why, when I found it tiresome in the first instance?"

Her expression darkened, and he glimpsed the real woman behind the false facade. "It would not be wise to rouse my ire. Perhaps I should leave, return to London and regale tales of the lady you intend to make your wife."

Max froze.

If she were a man, he would not stand for her petty threats. But he knew he had no option but to tread carefully.

"To what lady do you refer? I think you've spent too much time in the carriage, Catrina, and must be suffering from a distinct lack of air. I never said I intended to marry."

"You do not have to say anything." She gave an indolent wave. "When I heard of your little gathering, your intentions were clear. You want the inheritance. I cannot blame you for that. Indeed, I would be happy to help, safe in the knowledge that we could continue with our weekly rendezvous."

"Are you suggesting I should be unfaithful to my wife? If I had one, of course."

She shrugged. "I am suggesting you do not need to alter your life too drastically for the sake of being forced to marry to claim what is rightfully yours."

What the hell had he seen in her?

It wasn't as though he'd found the physical aspects of their relationship particularly satisfying. An image of his mother's ashen face flashed into his mind. Time and time again, his father humiliated her with his constant affairs. Max would be damned if he would behave in the same way.

"Call me naive," he snorted, "but I hope to remain faithful to my wife when I marry."

She could not hide her surprise. "I suppose her beauty is the obvious attraction. But when that fades what will you have then?"

A vision of Prudence wrestling with the plant pot, of her witty remarks and luscious lips, bombarded his thoughts. He could not pick one thing that attracted him to her. It was more a jumbled mix of delights packaged into a perfect parcel.

"Surprisingly, I am not that shallow. There is more to a woman than a pretty countenance."

Catrina gave a contemptuous snort. "And you expect me to believe you. You should have seen Mannerly's face when they greeted us at the door. It took him the best part of five minutes before he could close his mouth."

Max suppressed a frown. Catrina was speaking of Sarah Roxbury. He knew why she had made the assumption. Relief coursed through him. The error would give him a little time to decide what to do. Nonetheless, if he threw her out, she could ruin Sarah's chances of making a good match. And he refused to play the gallant knight forced to marry her as a means of saving her reputation.

"Of course, you know women as beautiful often lack passion when it comes to pleasing men," Catrina continued, patting her ebony locks. "As do women raised in the country."

Max chuckled to himself. Prudence was bursting with a fiery passion that made his cock ache just thinking about it. "Perhaps."

"I shall give you a week of married life before you're knocking on my door begging to come back."

Even after five years hard labour, her bed would be the last place he'd rest his head or any other part of his anatomy. Max bowed. "I shall leave you to change," he said with an air of indifference. "Dinner is served at seven. There—"

"I know," she said impatiently. "Your aunt bored us with the usual commentary. So, you're not throwing me out?"

Max chose not to respond. He walked to the door, turned to face her as his hand curled around the handle. "If you need anything, please do not hesitate to ask my aunt."

Stepping out into the hall, he closed the door behind him and paused for breath. What was supposed to be a relaxing weekend where he could spend more time with Miss Pickle, had turned into a covert operation to keep his ex-mistress under control.

God damn it. He would have Mannerly's hide for this. What the hell was the gentleman thinking? Prudence was far too sharp not to notice that his foul temper was a result of Mrs Beecham's surprising arrival. He would have no choice but to explain the situation. Perhaps he would have a quiet word with her after dinner once he had flayed Mannerly for his stupidity.

The next few hours passed without incident.

Max had not seen Prudence since the awkward meeting with Mrs Beecham. He suspected he owed her an apology for his frosty manner. But despite scouring the house, the lady was nowhere to be found.

Before everyone retired to their rooms to wash and change for dinner, they congregated in the drawing room to converse with the other guests.

Glancing around the room, he inclined his head to Mrs Shelby and her daughter, Miss Eunice Shelby, who sat on the sofa, sipping their tea. Mr Wyebourne was deep in conversation with Frederick Mannerly while Lucas Dempsey stood with his arms folded examining the portrait of a lady lounging on a chaise. Aunt Gwendoline entered with Sarah Roxbury, and they joined the other ladies to take refreshments.

"Still no word from Anthony?" Max said as he joined Lucas.

He had been good friends with Lucas and Anthony Dempsey for years. Both men were honest, sincere; they did not judge as others were wont to do.

"No. He's so preoccupied of late. It wouldn't surprise me if he'd forgotten what day it is."

Max had deliberately invited his friend in the hope Sarah's beauty would capture his interest enough to tear him away from the strains and stresses of responsibility.

"There's still time," Max said with a sigh. He scanned the room. Helena Dempsey and Prudence were absent. "It's my fault for trying to organise a gathering at such short notice. But I am keen to see Miss Roxbury introduced to a few notable people before my aunt whisks her away to London."

"I heard talk Catrina Beecham has arrived." There was a hint of reproof in Lucas' tone. "Is it wise to have your mistress at your home when entertaining family?"

"Catrina is no longer my mistress," Max whispered. "I have not seen her for a month or more. The blasted woman convinced Mannerly I'd invited her." Max glanced at the golden-haired giant. "The man is a simpleton. His head is so full of his own importance his brain is the size of a pea. But I fear Catrina is intent on wreaking havoc and will find a way to ruin things."

Lucas raised an arrogant brow. "Tell her to leave."

"What and watch her make a scene?" Max shook his head. "No."

"Then we will close ranks." Lucas grasped Max's shoulder to reinforce his offer of support. "It should not be too difficult to convince Mr Wyebourne to follow suit. And Helena is adept at putting ex-mistresses in their place."

"God, I'm glad you're here. It's important that everything goes smoothly."

Lucas glanced at the ladies seated on the sofa. "So, you're of a mind to marry."

Max groaned inwardly. Why did everyone assume he had developed a tendre for Sarah Roxbury? "Not at all. One cannot deny the lady has appeal. My aunt appears enamoured with her and has barely left her side. But while her beauty may captivate some men, it does nothing for me."

Lucas gave an arrogant grin. "I was not referring to the pretty fair-haired one, but to the one with a look of mischief in her eye and a tongue sharp enough to draw blood." He bent his head and whispered, "There is much more to be said for a woman with intelligence and wit. I should know. I married one."

Max blinked in shock at the gentleman's insight. Was his attraction to Prudence so obvious? The strange yearning filled his chest again: the need to delve deep and explore the passionate side of her nature.

"You know about the stipulations of my father's will?"

Lucas nodded. "You've mentioned it. Am I to assume that you intend to marry to claim your inheritance?"

Max leant closer. "I've but a few months until I turn thirty. While my father could not prevent me inheriting Roxbury Hall, I must marry before I can claim all of what's deemed rightfully mine."

Lucas frowned. "So, you're marrying for money," he reiterated coolly. "Let me give you some advice if I may, although you know how I hate to sound condescending. Marry for love. Nothing else gives the immense feeling of satisfaction that helps one sleep easier in their bed."

Max wasn't interested in sleeping. He had far more

amorous activities on his mind. "Not everyone is lucky enough to find what you have with Helena."

"I hate to tell you this, Max, but from where I'm standing you already have the look of a man besotted."

Before Max could form a reply, Prudence and Helena Dempsey entered the drawing room. After greeting his aunt and partaking in a brief conversation with Mrs Shelby, they came to join them.

"Ah, here you are. We were just talking about you," Lucas said in his usual arrogant drawl.

Panic flared in Max's chest. Lucas enjoyed teasing him and would no doubt say something to allude to his fondness for Prudence.

"What?" his wife began. "Were you saying how much you longed for our company?"

"Exactly so." Lucas nudged him. "What was it you said about Miss Roxbury?"

Max opened his mouth and then closed it again. He stared at Prudence, noting the coy smile playing on her lips. There was something different about her hair. This morning, it had been immaculately dressed by Anne, her previous maid. Now, loose tendrils had escaped from her coiffure to brush against her cheek; a few tickled her nape. The muscles in his abdomen clenched as he thought of running the tip of his tongue down the perfect column of her throat.

Max shook his head. "I said I owe her an apology for my miserable mood."

"It was rather a sudden shift," Prudence said with a look of mild surprise. "It is not good for the constitution for one's mood to fluctuate so dramatically. Perhaps you should head to Bath and take the waters. I hear all that hot steam works wonders for soothing the mind and body."

Max swallowed. Had he imagined the seductive lilt to her tone?

"I know of many ways to soothe the mind and body without venturing all the way to Bath," he replied.

The tip of her tongue moistened the seam of her lips. "Then you must enlighten me, my lord."

Lucas Dempsey cleared his throat as he nodded discreetly at the door.

Max had almost forgotten Catrina had come to the manor. When she sauntered into the drawing room arm-in-arm with Prudence's grandfather, panic and a deep sense of foreboding gripped him by the throat.

Brazenly, Catrina walked over to them. "Look who I found wandering the corridors." Her innocent smile did not detract from the devilish twinkle in her eye.

Prudence struggled to suppress a gasp. "Grandpapa, I thought you were resting in your room." Her gaze fell to his crumpled cravat and Max noted a blush rise to her cheeks.

"You can imagine my surprise when I found him marching back and forth along the landing. He seemed a little confused and muttered strangely to himself, so I thought he must surely be in desperate need of company." Catrina turned to the old man as she clutched his arm, failing to prevent the wicked glint in her eyes from reaching her lips. "Perhaps a cup of tea might settle your nerves."

"Tea? Tea?" Mr Hargrove gasped and spluttered. "You want me to drink tea when the grenadiers could surround us at any moment? Good Lord, no. We need to be on our guard, need to stay alert."

Catrina gave a mocking chuckle. "You make it sound as though we are at war, sir, that the house is about to be surrounded by a blood-thirsty battalion."

"Come, I shall take you back to your room." Prudence spoke calmly though fiddled with her fingers. "You're not well."

"Oh, he cannot sit up there all day," Catrina protested.

"Not when his granddaughter is proving to be such entertaining company." She glanced at the sofa. "I'm sure Mrs Shelby would love to hear all about the dreadful invasion that has the militia camped near the grounds of the castle."

"Hush now, girl," the old man said as his nervous gaze scanned the room. "Would you have everyone know of the captain's business? Spies lurk everywhere, even in the unlikeliest of places."

"You may take comfort in the knowledge, Mr Hargrove, that there are no spies here," Max reassured. "I can promise you that."

"Let us take some air, Grandpapa." Prudence glared at Catrina before returning her attention to her grandfather. "We can scour the perimeter, be on the lookout for anything suspicious."

The old man's eyes grew wide, and he sucked in a breath. "But it's not safe out there."

Max could see Prudence was struggling to maintain her composure. He admired the fact she had not tried to disguise the man's obvious problem but had put her grandfather's needs before her own fears of embarrassment. A few of the other guests were gaping in their direction, whispering amongst themselves. Max had to do something to help.

He tugged the sleeve of Lucas' coat, turned away from the group and whispered, "Just go along with whatever I say no matter how ridiculous it sounds."

Lucas raised a curious brow but nodded.

"I have not yet had the chance to introduce you to Captain Lawrence," Max said, waving a hand at Lucas. "He has called today to reassure us all is well. Isn't that right, Captain?"

Suppressing a brief look of shock, Lucas smiled confidently and squared his shoulders. "I have come to put your minds at ease. Indeed, I intend to visit regularly over the course of the weekend."

"What on earth are you talking about?" Catrina scoffed. "Mr Dempsey is not Captain Lawrence."

"Not Captain Lawrence?" The old man jumped to attention, fiddled with his spectacles and narrowed his gaze as he scanned Lucas' impeccable attire. "Why are you not in uniform, Captain?"

"Precisely," Catrina mocked. "Where is your uniform, Mr Dempsey?"

Lucas bent his head. "Only a civilian would ask such a ridiculous question. Obviously, I do not wish to draw attention to myself. If there are spies in our midst, I will root them out before they have time to report back to headquarters. Perhaps you would care to accompany me on a tour of the grounds, Mr Hargrove." He glanced at Catrina with disdain before addressing the old man once more. "Have a sharp eye mind. Evil lurks all around us."

Prudence's grandfather straightened, gaining a sudden air of importance. "Oh, well, if you think I can be of some help, Captain."

"Let's be off then." Lucas inclined his head to the group. "Rest assured, we will report back within the hour."

Max watched his friend escort the old man out of the drawing room. "I must say, Lucas is remarkably talented, as is your grandfather, Miss Roxbury. Their acting skills far surpass mine. What an entertaining idea of yours, Mrs Dempsey."

Mrs Dempsey smiled. "I know. We were at a house party recently, and the host assigned all the guests roles to play. I had to convince everyone I'd seen a ghost. Acting is not as easy as my husband makes it look."

Prudence's smile conveyed a genuine look of affection and appreciation. "I wonder who will be next."

"No one told me about the game," Catrina said with a sulky pout.

"Did they not?" Max suppressed a chuckle at the thought of Catrina being relegated to play the role of a scullery maid. "I shall have a word with my aunt and make sure she puts a card in your chamber."

"Had someone mentioned it," Catrina huffed, "I would have known what to look for. But then your mind was rather occupied when you escorted me to my room."

Max clenched his teeth before feigning a smile. "I suggest you look again before I put my aunt to any trouble."

"What a good idea," Mrs Dempsey said. "Who knows? Perhaps you will play the bitter mistress, Mrs Beecham, aggrieved at being discarded for a much younger and prettier model. Perhaps you will have to be vicious and vindictive as a way to get attention."

Max dared not breathe. He didn't know whether to laugh or cry. It was probably the most scathing insult he had ever heard from a woman's lips. Catrina could say nothing. The clever way Helena had delivered the jibe, made it impossible to prove the remarks were intended to be malicious. Of course, it also meant that Prudence now knew the nature of his relationship with Catrina.

Catrina's cheeks turned berry red. "It could be worse. I could play the wife of the most scandalous man in England."

Helena Dempsey appeared unperturbed by the comment. "I doubt that. Only someone who did not know you would assume you were wife material. And Lucas would never be attracted to someone so disingenuous."

Prudence pursed her lips. "Would anyone care for any refreshments?"

Catrina said nothing, but her eyes looked like they could spit fiery flames. She raised her chin with an air of hauteur and flounced out of the room.

"Heavens," Prudence said a little breathlessly. "You were all remarkable." She took Helena Dempsey's hand and squeezed it. "Please tell your husband I am eternally grateful for his assistance."

The lady smiled and fanned her face with her hand. "I will. He was pretty remarkable if I say so myself. Indeed, I think I have fallen in love with him all over again."

Max removed his pocket watch and checked the time. "We have an hour before we need to change for dinner. Shall we all take a stroll in the garden? We can search for Lucas and your grandfather."

"I think I'll rest in my room before dinner," Helena Dempsey said. "If you see Lucas, tell him I am waiting for him upstairs."

Max could tell by the twinkle in the lady's eye that she had no desire to rest. "Certainly." He inclined his head and turned his attention to Prudence. "Shall we take a turn about the garden?"

"I would like nothing more, my lord."

There it was again, that soft, seductive timbre that held a wealth of promise. His thoughts took a sudden serious turn as he realised he would need to explain Catrina Beecham's arrival. Perhaps he should hint at the possibility of marriage. He stared at her lips. The hue appeared a little pinker than he remembered. Then again, perhaps he should kiss the lady until she submitted.

CHAPTER 8

Lord Roxbury escorted Prue out into the garden. She felt oddly nervous considering the fact she had been alone with him on numerous occasions. The hour spent in Mrs Dempsey's company had been interesting. Helena was far too perceptive when it came to matters of the heart. Coupled with her straight-talking, it had not taken much for Prue to confess all.

"I think I should begin by apologising for my frosty mood earlier," Lord Roxbury said as they descended the stone steps leading to the gravel path. "After Mrs Dempsey's comments in the drawing room, I assume you understand why I was, and still am, so damnably annoyed."

Prue recalled Helena's words: gentlemen did not want to hear lies or feigned titters. Above all else, a lady should always be honest, and true to herself.

"Mrs Beecham is your mistress. That much is obvious." Indeed, while she had initially struggled with the thought, it pleased her to know the woman only roused negative feelings. Nonetheless, it still didn't explain why she had come.

"She is not my mistress, Prue," he said sharply, yet her heart raced at the sound of her given name falling so easily from his lips. "I have been acquainted with her in the past, yes. But I ended any arrangement we had, months ago."

"Has she come here hoping for a chance to warm your bed?" It was not the sort of question a lady should ask a gentleman, but Prue spoke in a playful tone that helped mask any jealousy she felt at the prospect.

He sighed and brushed his hand through his hair. "I will not lie to you. Yes, she came hoping to become reacquainted."

"But you did not invite her here?"

"Of course not."

She could feel his assessing gaze searching her face, but she pretended to admire the rose bushes. As they came to the end of the path, Mr Dempsey and her grandfather appeared from the maze.

"You neglected to mention you had a maze," Mr Dempsey said in a languid tone as they came to meet them. "I must confess, despite all my military training, I would still be wandering around in there had it not been for Mr Hargrove."

Her grandfather chuckled. "It is purely a matter of logic, Captain. One must be systematic in their methods. Picking a path at random serves to make the task more difficult." He turned to Prue and tapped her affectionately on the arm. "It's all safe in there, dear girl. We've searched the garden. Haven't we, Captain Lawrence?"

Mr Dempsey smiled, his handsome countenance causing her to suck in a breath. One could not help but admire perfection.

"We have," Mr Dempsey agreed. "And now I must return to my duties."

Lord Roxbury raised a brow. "I believe you have a few duties to attend to in your chamber. As much as we are grateful for your company, one's responsibilities must take precedence."

Mr Dempsey glanced up at a window on the first floor. A sinful smile touched his lips. "Thank you. I shall attend to my duties at once."

"Thank you, Captain Lawrence," Prue said with genuine gratitude, "for assisting us during these trying times."

"You're most welcome." His amused gaze drifted to Lord Roxbury. "I shall escort Mr Hargrove to his room and will call in on him frequently over the next few days. He's challenged me to a game of chess."

"Oh, you have done more than enough already," Prue implored. "We shall escort him back to the house."

"It would be a shame for the two of you not to partake in a leisurely stroll while it is still warm out," Mr Dempsey replied. "Besides, I have assured Mr Hargrove that I will search his chamber."

Grandpapa nodded. "I shall rest easy once the captain has conducted his investigation." He turned to Mr Dempsey and wagged his finger. "Now, there's no need to question Henry. I would trust that boy with my life."

"Then let us go and meet him. England needs more dependable young men." Mr Dempsey inclined his head, and both men marched off towards the house.

Prue watched them until they mounted the steps, her hand resting on her heart as she breathed a sigh. "There are not many gentlemen as kind and good-natured as Mr Dempsey. No wonder his wife is so hopelessly in love with him."

"Most people do not get the opportunity to witness that side of his character," Lord Roxbury said. "For a long time, people believed him to be the worst sort of scoundrel."

Prue gasped. "Then they are obviously dolts and dunces."

Lord Roxbury laughed. "I must admit to being somewhat

jealous of your admiration for Mr Dempsey," he said as he offered his arm. She accepted the gentlemanly gesture, and they walked towards the maze.

"I'm of the opinion all good deeds should not go unnoticed, that is all." Prue knew she should use the opportunity to be honest with him. "But you shouldn't be jealous. I do not admire him in the same way I admire you."

There, she had followed Helena's advice and spoken from the heart. Indeed, while others might find her forward approach scandalous, she found it quite liberating.

"Then I must have done something wonderful to win your high esteem."

Seduced by the excitement caused by such flirtatious banter, she said, "I'm afraid I'm shallow and find your warm lips have helped to win you favour."

She could feel his penetrating gaze and so tried to maintain her confident composure.

"Then perhaps we should attempt to navigate the maze," he said. His playful tone carried a hint of desire. "Although this time, you must promise to wait for me."

The tickling in her stomach fluttered through her body at the realisation that she wanted him to kiss her again. But even with her complete lack of experience, she knew she wanted more than that from him.

"I promise to stay with you for the duration." She turned and offered him her brightest smile. "If you can keep my interest."

"I've never told you, but when you smile your beauty is breathtaking. If I could, I would make it my mission to rouse the same look every day for the rest of my life."

Prue swallowed down the sudden rush of desire his compliment unleashed. No one had ever spoken to her so openly or with such affection. The warmth filling her chest travelled lower to pool between her thighs and her intimate place pulsed to its own lustful beat. Once safely concealed behind the giant topiary hedges of the maze, the ropes of constraint slipped away, and she felt free to express herself.

"While your compliments warm my heart," she purred, "they are not what makes me want you."

He stopped abruptly, turned to face her, blinked numerous times as his breath came quicker. "Don't tease me, Prue," he said, disregarding all propriety again to use her given name. "This morning you told me you had no wish to experience another silly moment of madness. Now, from your words and the seductive timbre of your voice, you give me hope that you may have changed your mind."

"Perhaps I have changed my mind," she said coyly. Indeed, his kindness and generosity, his sinful mouth and wicked hands, all made for an enticing combination.

"What are you saying?" His hazel eyes flashed with excitement. "Are you saying you want me to kiss you again?"

Feeling empowered by her boldness, Prue moistened her lips, deliberately increased the depth of her breathing so that her chest heaved enough to draw his gaze. While lacking experience in the art of seduction, she was more than determined to outshine Catrina Beecham.

"I'm saying ... you will have to catch me to find out."

Without another word, she hiked up the hem of her pretty dress and ran along the narrow aisle. If she could just reach the end before he caught up with her, he would be forced to choose between two paths. With a jubilant chuckle, she raced around the corner, taking the left turn which led to a dead end as opposed to the other path leading to the exit.

As she hid in the depths of the small square-shaped recess that led to nowhere, she covered her mouth with her hand to prevent another chuckle from escaping. She would leave everything to the hands of Fate. If he found her, she would kiss him with every aching fibre of her being. If not, then ... well ... she would have to find him and kiss him, regardless.

When she heard the pad of footsteps retreating, disappointment flooded her chest. What had seemed like a good idea, now made her feel foolish and naive — no match for a mistress. With a heavy sigh, she took the few steps necessary to rejoin the path.

Before she knew what was happening, strong arms enveloped her and pushed her back against the green topiary wall.

"Caught you," Lord Roxbury said. His sensual tone caused the hairs at her nape to tingle.

"Heavens, you ... you scared me half to death." Amidst breathless pants, she became increasingly aware of his hard body pressed against hers. His earthy masculine scent made her feel dizzy, a little drunk with desire. Compelled to do the only thing her mind and body would allow, she reached up and grabbed the lapels of his coat, pulled his head to hers and kissed him scandalously.

Lord Roxbury did not protest.

In a matter of seconds, what had begun as soft caressing movements and tender strokes of the tongue, turned into a frantic lust-fuelled frenzy. His hands were everywhere all at once. She could not taste him deeply enough to satisfy the clawing need consuming her. She clutched at his shoulders, then threaded her fingers through his hair as he thrust wildly into her mouth.

His potent masculine scent filled her head; his warm, wet lips held her captive. When he moaned into her mouth, she whimpered in response.

"Max," she panted as he moved to nuzzle and nip the sensitive spot on her neck. Waves of pure pleasure rippled down to her toes until she became lost in a blissful paradise of passion.

"God, Prue, you make me insane with need."

"Just kiss me," she muttered, tilting her head to give him full access.

Prue writhed against him, desperate to feel the warmth of his body, desperate to sate a craving she could not define. Her breasts felt heavy; her nipples ached as they pressed against the layers of fabric. The fire in her belly raged hot, scorching.

All the lonely nights that lay before her vanished in an instant and she imagined spending every moment encased in his strong arms.

"I need to be inside you," he whispered, thrusting against her. The muscles in her core pulsed in response. "I need to feel you hugging me tightly."

His crude words should have shocked her, but they only heightened her pleasure. "Tell me again. Tell me what you need."

A sinful grin played at the corners his mouth. He brushed his lips across hers as his hands snaked up under her dress to caress her bare thighs. "I need to touch you." He kissed her once, long and deep, an act of possession. "I want to hear you say my name as you beg for me to end your torment."

"Yes," she breathed as his fingers brushed the intimate place exposed to him. "Tell me more."

"I want to watch you sit astride me," he whispered against her ear, sucking the lobe before adding, "watch you take me deep, watch your eyes glaze as I fill you full."

Prue could hardly breathe. It all sounded so wanton, so reckless, so wonderful. In her mind, she imagined lying naked on the grass, as she succumbed to his urgent demands. "I want you, Max." The words drifted from her lips.

"Bloody hell." His curse conveyed his frustration. He pulled away. "If … if I don't stop now, I won't stop until I've made you mine."

Prue blinked, tried to latch on to a shred of logic amidst all the wicked thoughts of carnal pleasures. "Good Lord, I am struggling to think clearly."

He chuckled yet she could feel the ravenous need radiating from him. "I want you in my bed, Prue. Now. Tonight. And every night hereafter."

"By now, you should know I don't give a fig for propriety." Her head still felt light and giddy. The moist place between her legs still ached for his touch. "But I cannot conduct an illicit liaison knowing it would greatly affect my sister's chances of making a decent match."

He lowered his head and kissed her again, the fierce passion that existed between them flaming within seconds.

"Marry me, Prue," he demanded as he broke away with a hungry gasp. "Marry me and become the mistress of Hagley Manor."

She should have been ecstatic at the prospect of returning home, at the prospect of marrying a man she desired and admired greatly. But he had made no mention of love. It was a ridiculous dream to think such a thing was possible at her age and with her complete lack of connections.

"Why?" she muttered.

Quickly disguising the nervous look in his eyes, he said, "The level of passion that exists between us is rare indeed. I enjoy your company immensely. I find you witty, intelligent, and utterly beguiling."

"But we do not love one another."

"No. Not yet, but I hope that will change." His honest reply gave her confidence that they could develop deep feelings over time, and she desperately wanted to be close to him. "If we were married, would we share the same bed? Would you reside here with me?"

His eyes grew wide with astonishment. "Of course. As I

said, I intended to worship your body by night, and worship your mind by day."

Prue knew it was the only offer she would ever get. It would be the only chance of her having a home and a family of her own. She would not sell her soul for such luxuries, but she cared for Lord Roxbury. She found him fascinating, funny, and sinfully handsome. If she spent a lifetime searching, she doubted she would find a man who could make her body burn with desire.

"Then my answer is yes."

He blinked. "You're sure you do not need more time to consider my proposal?"

She grabbed his lapels, pulled him closer and devoured his mouth once more. "No," she eventually said, swallowing down a gasp as she drew her lips from his. She would just have to hope Helena was right when she said the lord appeared besotted with her. "I have made my decision."

"Were you persuaded by my consummate skill as a seducer?"

Prue raised an arrogant brow. "I think you will find you're the one who has been ravished and seduced, my lord."

He gave a mischievous grin. "Perhaps you're right, Miss Pickle, yet the weekend is far from over."

CHAPTER 9

Prue hardly slept a wink that night. Thankfully, she was sharing a room with Sarah. Otherwise, she would have been far too weak to forbid the amorous lord entrance.

Sarah was delighted to hear the news of their betrothal. As was customary, Max had sought permission from her grandfather, who appeared to comprehend him fully. Of course, it also meant Captain Lawrence would need to call again at Hagley Manor, and her grandfather had been thoroughly pleased at the prospect. They decided to break the news to his aunt as soon as the guests departed.

"I am so thrilled for you, Prue," Sarah said as they sat alone in the dining room, eating breakfast. She picked up a piece of toast from the rack. "And to think you will be mistress of our family home. Mother would have been overjoyed."

"I can't help but feel a little guilty." Prue poured another cup of tea. "We were supposed to find you a husband this weekend."

Sarah shook her head. "The intention was that I would feel more relaxed when in company. And I do. Gwendoline assures me I will love it in London and has offered to act as chaperone for the duration of my stay."

Prue gave a sigh of contentment. "I keep expecting to wake up and find it has all been a wonderful dream. Even when I came here hoping Max would agree to help us, I never imagined it would all work out so well."

"What about Grandpapa? If I go to stay in London with Gwendoline, will you take care of him and the girls?"

Prue nodded. "I spoke to Max about it last night," she said, although they had done more than talk when locked in his study at midnight. A smile touched her lips as she recalled sitting on his lap, running her hands up under his shirt to touch hot molten skin. "You will all come and live here, and we'll put tenants in the cottage."

Sarah placed her cup on the saucer. "The girls will be ecstatic."

"Don't say anything to anyone. Other than Grandpapa, you're the only person we've told."

"I won't." Sarah glanced at the mantel clock. "I'm to accompany Gwendoline and some other members of the party to Tonbridge. To see if any improvements have been made to the castle. It seems the gentlemen are keen to see the medieval structure and decided the fresh air will do us all the world of good."

"How do you find Lord Mannerly and Mr Wyebourne? Could you see either of them as potential suitors?"

Sarah scrunched up her nose and shook her head. "No, not at all. Mr Wyebourne is extremely sweet-natured, and Lord Mannerly comes out with the most ridiculous things, one can't help but laugh. When I look at them, I do not get the tickles in my tummy or the fluttering in my breast that I've heard tale of." She sighed. "I'm sure Fate will conspire to throw me into the path of a handsome, brooding gentleman who will set my heart aflame."

Just thinking about Max Roxbury caused Prue to feel all the things Sarah mentioned, including a hot pulsing in a rather intimate place. Her heart swelled at the thought of spending time in his company. Prue resisted the need to go in search of him, to ease the growing need that was all consuming.

"Lord Harwood is yet to arrive. Perhaps he will race up the drive on his charger like a gallant knight of old and rescue you from the company of dullards."

Sarah chuckled as she placed her napkin on the table and stood. "You do have a vivid imagination, Prue, but I doubt his lordship would travel all this way just for a day."

Prue shrugged. "Stranger things have happened. Look at me. Your sensible, rational sister has turned into a sentimental wreck. Who would have thought it possible?"

Sarah tilted her head and smiled. "You've always had a huge heart, Prue. You were just waiting for a chance to fall in love."

Had she fallen in love with Max Roxbury?

She was extremely fond of him. Even when awake, she would dream of being enveloped in his strong, warm arms.

"You'd best hurry along," Prue said, as she did not wish to sit there all day trying to analyse her feelings. "Gwendoline will think you've changed your mind about going."

Sarah came over and kissed her on the cheek. "I'll check on Grandpapa and the girls before I leave. Sit here a while longer and enjoy the peace."

Prue sat alone, wondering if her parents would have approved of her hasty decision to marry a man she had known for a little less than a month. In a bid to stop thinking, she had another slice of toast as there was no one to accuse her of being greedy.

The soft pad of footsteps caught her attention, and she

glanced up to see Catrina Beecham saunter into the dining room.

"Good morning, Miss Roxbury," she said with her usual haughty air. She lifted various lids on the silver serving dishes lined up on the sideboard, tutted and grumbled before replacing them with a clatter. "I think I shall just have toast. The bacon looks too dry and the eggs are far too runny."

Despite knowing Max had no interest in the woman, Prue could not stop various licentious images from flooding her mind. Had Max kissed Catrina Beecham in the same way he'd kissed her? Had he whispered amorous endearments in her ear? Had she meant more to him than his angry countenance conveyed?

"Will you not be joining the others on their trip to Tonbridge?" Prue asked in an attempt to be civil. She understood Max's reasons for not throwing the woman out. Protecting Sarah's reputation was more important than the need to ease her own feelings of jealousy.

Catrina Beecham sat down opposite her. She sighed as she scanned the two pieces of cold toast sitting in the rack. "I have no interest in visiting old relics. Forgive my bluntness, but I find their conversation tiresome. Mrs Shelby talks of nothing other than her daughter's musical accomplishments and Mannerly cannot recall what day it is, let alone anything else."

"I'm surprised you came knowing you would be surrounded by such utter bores." Prue smiled though inside she imagined emptying the teapot over the woman's head.

"One particular attraction has made the visit more bearable. After Mrs Dempsey's comment, I am sure you're aware the reason for my invitation." Mrs Beecham bit into the toast, wincing at the crunching sound. She threw it down onto her plate. "Good heavens, Roxbury should get his house in order before he invites guests to stay."

Prue inhaled deeply. She thought of pretty flowers and green meadows to ease her irritation. "I hope your accommodation is proving to be satisfactory. I assisted Lord Roxbury in allocating the rooms. Indeed, he had no notion you were coming."

"Well, under the circumstances, I doubt it is something he considered fit to mention to an innocent lady." She tucked a stray black curl behind her ear before examining her empty teacup. "Please tell me there is tea in the pot." She gave a weak smile as she poured. "A gentleman does not discuss his private affairs. Least not with the family of the lady he intends to marry."

Prue struggled to hide her surprise. "Lord Roxbury has spoken to you of his plans to marry?"

"Of course," she said, thrusting her nose in the air. "Surely you are not silly enough to believe he will remain faithful to your sister. It requires more than beauty to keep a man's interest."

It was apparent Mrs Beecham knew nothing other than what her cunning, devious little mind had concocted.

"You would be advised to warn your sister as to the true nature of her prospective husband," Mrs Beecham added, "should she be under any misconception."

Catrina Beecham really was the most spiteful and vindictive of creatures. Prue felt like slapping Max Roxbury for his blindness and utter stupidity. Indeed, anger burned inside. Despite numerous efforts to douse the flames, it continued to rage within.

"I think you are the one suffering from a misconception. Clearly, Lord Roxbury has said nothing to you about his intentions else you would not have made the obvious error." Prue exhaled, feeling remarkably better. She glanced at the door and noticed Helena Dempsey hovering, unsure whether to come in.

Mrs Beecham sat back in the chair, folded her arms across her chest and scanned Prue with an air of disdain. "Well, aren't I the fool. But then it was an easy mistake to make. I should have known that desperate men often look for the simplest solution to their problem. Looking at you, it all makes much more sense now."

Without a prompt, Helena marched into the room. "Good morning, Miss Roxbury. How delightful you look. Your complexion is positively glowing, no wonder his lordship can't take his eyes off you." Helena came and sat next to Prue. "Ah, Mrs Beecham, I didn't notice you there. Isn't it a little early for you, or were you struggling to find your way to your own chamber?"

Mrs Beecham huffed. "Any bed would be preferable to the one you sleep in. One must lie there at night wondering if they will still be breathing come the morning."

No doubt the woman was referring to Mr Dempsey's scandalous past.

"Well, it appears you are intent on trying out as many beds as you can in a bid to find one that proves satisfactory." Helena turned to Prue and smiled. "More tea, Miss Roxbury?"

"I would rather be free to see whom I choose than to know a gentleman is only marrying me to claim his inheritance." Mrs Beecham focused her attention on Prue, put her hand to her breast and feigned surprise. "What? Did you not know of the clause that forbids Lord Roxbury inheriting anything not entailed? Unless he marries within the next three months, he loses everything. And so it seems you, too, Miss Roxbury, are suffering from an embarrassing misconception."

It took a moment for Prue to absorb Mrs Beecham's words. She recalled the way Max had kissed her so passionately, all the things he had said. Her heart raced as she considered the possibility that the woman spoke the truth.

"What a very sad creature you are, Mrs Beecham." Helena stood abruptly. "How very lonely it must be to have no husband, to know that men only use you for their own gain, to be the ugly stain on every decent lady's slipper."

Mrs Beecham glared at her.

"Now it seems I have lost my appetite," Helena continued, "and you are obviously so enamoured with yourself we feel as though we are intruding on a lovers' tryst. Come, Miss Roxbury, let us go where the air is a little more pleasant."

Prue had no desire to speak to Mrs Beecham again. It took a tremendous amount of effort not to drag her off her chair and kick her scrawny backside all the way back to London. As Prue neared the door, it suddenly occurred to her that Mrs Beecham would always look for ways to be unkind and malicious. Even if she did stay for the entire weekend, nothing would stop the woman spitting her venomous remarks to all who would listen.

Prue stopped abruptly. "When you have finished your tea, Mrs Beecham, you are to go to your room and pack. I shall speak to Lord Roxbury, who will arrange transport back to London. I'll be damned before I let you stay another day in this house."

Mrs Beecham's eyes widened. Her mouth fell open, and she snapped it shut. "Don't you think you are running away with yourself? You are not the mistress of the house yet, my dear."

Prue took a step towards her. "Perhaps I did not make myself clear. If you do not leave this house today, I will be forced to drag you out. Rest assured, should I hear tales of your vicious gossip, as Lady Roxbury, I shall be forced to rally supporters to belittle you wherever you go."

She did not give the woman a chance to retaliate but left

the room with Helena Dempsey.

"You were marvellous." Helena put her hand on Prue's arm. "Ignore her. She wants the gentleman for herself and will do whatever it takes to achieve her goal. I have seen her like before."

Despite Mrs Beecham's bitter comments, Prue suspected there was a grain of truth to her words. "Have you heard mention of any clauses to his father's will?"

Helena shook her head. "No. Even if it is true, I have seen the way Lord Roxbury looks at you. I know the tone and intonation of a man desperately in love. But you should go to him, ask him to be honest with you."

Prue nodded. "I will. I must know why he has asked me to marry him."

Helena's eyes grew wide. "So he *has* asked you to marry him. How wonderful. I knew it the moment I saw you both together."

"Please, don't tell anyone. We have yet to mention it to his aunt, and she would be dreadfully upset to be the last to know."

Helena tapped her finger to her lips. "I won't breathe a word. Come and find me when you've spoken to him. Either way, you may need to talk."

Prue thanked her and went off in search of Max. She suspected he would be in his study. Picturing the room brought memories of the previous night's amorous activities flooding back. For the first time in her life, she had opened her heart to the possibility of love. Now that the warm feeling blossomed in her chest she could not stop it from flourishing.

But what if it had been nothing more than a foolish dream?

What if every word from his lips turned out to be a wicked lie?

CHAPTER 10

Max was supposed to be examining the list of repairs he needed to make to the estate. With most of the guests heading to Tonbridge, he had decided to spend an hour putting a few things in order. He had got as far as reading the line informing him the roof on the carriage house leaked during heavy rainstorms, before his thoughts drifted back to Prudence.

Glancing at the chaise near the bookcase, he recalled the way her eager hands had explored the muscles in his chest. She had worn one of Madame Duval's exquisite creations to dinner. The short, full sleeves were designed to sit low on the shoulders, which offered a gentleman the advantage of sliding them down easily to reveal soft mounds of creamy-white flesh.

A knock on the door disturbed his erotic musings.

Damn.

He called for the person to enter, his mood dramatically improving when he realised the object of his desire came in to stand before him. One look at her irate expression told him something was most definitely amiss.

"Have you come to continue with your lesson in enlightenment?" He hoped his languorous tone would help her to forget whatever trifle had roused her ire.

"In a manner of speaking."

Max sucked in a breath as his cock jerked in response. By the time they'd had the banns read, and arranged all other necessaries needed for a wedding, it would be a month before he could have her in his bed. Then again, if they procured a common licence from the bishop and married in the parish, they could speed the process up considerably.

"Well?" She placed her hands on her hips. "Is it true?"

Feeling a sudden sense of foreboding, he sat back in the chair. "Is what true?"

"That you must marry to claim your inheritance."

Bloody hell.

He would bet every guinea he had that Catrina had opened her mouth. Max jumped to his feet. He marched over to close the door and then turned to face her.

"Yes," he said with some apprehension. "That part is true but—"

"I knew it." She turned away from him and began muttering to herself. He touched her on the shoulder. "Don't," she said as she swung back around. Pain and disappointment welled in her eyes. "Why didn't you tell me from the beginning? You've made me look a complete fool. What was it that swayed you? The fact that I'm deemed too plain to attract a man's eye, and so you took pity on me, or that you thought I would be desperate to accept?"

Max frowned. "None of those things. Will you not let me explain?"

She waved her hand wildly in the air. "Go on. I would like to hear why you chose to use me as a means to fill your coffers."

He had a strange feeling nothing he could say would

placate her. Still, he had to try. "Everything I told you about my father was true. No. I did not mention the cruel stipulations he made to his will. Until I came here, I wasn't sure what I wanted to do."

She snorted. "Until you found someone foolish enough to believe your fake protestations you mean."

"Until I found someone I cared for deeply enough to want to marry." He took a step forward, and she took a step back. "My mother married for convenience, and she paid for it every day of her life." Old feelings of bitterness infused his tone. "I could not live like that. I refuse to live like that. I care for you, Prue. Surely after our interlude in the maze, after what happened later in here, you must know I could not possibly fake such depth of passion."

Prue shook her head. "I don't know what to think. I don't know if I can trust you."

Frustration turned to anger. "You're the one with the most to gain. Perhaps you only agreed to marry me so you could move back to your precious manor." He knew as soon as the words left his lips that he had made a stupid mistake.

She gaped at him. "If you believe me to be so shallow, then why on earth did you ask me to be your wife?"

Because I think I'm in love with you.

Hell and damnation. He'd almost let the words fall from his lips. Fear made him hesitate. He would not make a declaration without knowing for sure. "Why did you consent?" he retorted, dragging his hand through his hair.

She straightened her spine and raised her chin. "Because at that point, I didn't know you'd lied to me."

"God, Prue, I haven't lied to you. I simply chose not to divulge something I thought might cause you to doubt me."

"Then forgive me if I used the wrong word. You deceived me, Max. You deliberately kept it from me, and now your mistress has just sat at the dining table and humiliated me in front of Helena Dempsey."

"God damn it, Prue. Mrs Beecham is not my mistress." He threw his hands in the air. "I shall insist she leaves the manor at once if that will make you happy."

"You're too late," she said in a condescending tone that only served to fuel his anger. "I have already told Catrina Beecham that if she doesn't leave today, I will personally drag her out of here."

Good Lord. Max didn't know whether he was delighted she had the gumption to tackle the woman, or annoyed he'd not done so in the beginning.

"We will just have to hope she does not cause any problems for Sarah."

"Trust me." Prue raised her chin. "That woman will keep her tongue else I shall not be held responsible for the consequences."

Max could feel a smile forming at the corners of his mouth. He couldn't help it. He admired her more now than he had when she was prepared to wrestle a man over her mother's roses. She was damnably attractive when angry. All he could think about was plundering her mouth for the riches he knew lay buried inside.

A tap on the door distracted him. The person did not wait for a response before storming in.

Max groaned when he noted Catrina Beecham standing there.

"Can I speak to you for a moment," she said in her usual lofty tone.

Before he could open his mouth, Prue stomped over to the door. "I shall leave you to your business," she said, and then disappeared into the hall.

Max stared at the open door for a few seconds, his mind in turmoil. "What is it, Catrina?"

"I came to offer an apology and to say goodbye." She took a step towards him. Knowing her to be somewhat unpredictable, he waved to the chair, while he moved to sit behind his desk.

"You should not have come here." He folded his arms across his chest as he was struggling to sit and listen when all he wanted to do was to comfort Prudence. "We were friends who happened—"

"We were more than friends, Max," she interjected with a chuckle.

"We *were*," he acknowledged, stressing the past tense. "But I am to be married."

"Given the circumstances of your father's—"

He held up his hand to prevent her from continuing. "I am marrying Miss Roxbury because I care for her deeply. It has nothing to do with claiming my inheritance, and I insist you refrain from making any comments to the contrary."

Catrina narrowed her brows, shook her head and scrunched her nose. "You expect me to believe you care for Miss Roxbury? I know you're lying, Max. I could understand why you would marry the pretty one but—"

"There must be something wrong with your eyes, Catrina. I suggest you consider getting spectacles on your return to London." Max stood abruptly. The sharp sound of the chair scraping the boards conveyed his disdain. The need to defend Prudence burned inside. "Perhaps I should enlighten you to a few facts regarding the wants and desires of men."

She snorted. "I know enough of men to know what pleases them. I know enough of lords to know what they want."

"I highly doubt it." Max gave a wry smirk. "Would you like me to tell you what every lord wants, what I want?" He did not give her an opportunity to answer. "I want a woman who has depth of character, not the superficial pomp I'm used to. I want a woman who will fight for her family even if it means disagreeing with those popular in society. I want a woman who inflames my heart and soul rather than just one part of my anatomy, whose inner grace illuminates her features so that her beauty is blinding. In short, Mrs Beecham, I want Prudence Roxbury."

Catrina swallowed visibly. Her mouth opened and closed a few times as she struggled to form a reply. "I see."

"Now," he began, placing his hands flat on the desk. "I suggest you pack your things this instant. My coachman will see you safely back to London."

"Your coachman has taken a party to Tonbridge. I shall keep to my room and travel home this evening." She inclined her head. "With your permission, of course."

"Agreed. But I don't want to see you until it's time for you to depart." He waved his hand to the door, the gesture conveying his intention.

Catrina stood. "I know it's not the right time to say this, but I care for you, Max."

"No, you don't. You never did. The sad thing is you're afraid of being alone and so cling on to anyone who can fill the void." He noticed the muscle in her jaw twitch as her gaze darkened, and so added, "Coming here was highly inappropriate. It speaks of someone desperate for company, someone who is unhappy and lonely."

She flicked her head: a sign she refused to accept his opinion. "Do not presume to know me just because we have been intimate. I much prefer my own company than to sit around drinking tea, gossiping and boasting of my accomplishments. I enjoy the physical aspects of men but do not wish to lumber myself with a husband."

The conversation was going nowhere. "Then there is

nothing more to say. I shall send word when it is time to leave."

Catrina smiled yet her cold eyes conveyed an entirely different emotion. "Goodbye, Max."

Max watched her flounce out through the door. He swung around and punched the air to release his frustration. He knew he should search for Prudence, to explain things in a better way. The inner voice he often ignored told him to give her time to think, time to reflect on all he had said. Only then could they have an honest, frank discussion regarding their future.

With a sigh, he flopped down into the chair. Thank heavens he did not have to spend the day entertaining guests. His aunt's suggestion of a trip out had come at the perfect time. Glancing at the architrave on the opposite wall, he jumped up and went to explore the secret room. The room was now empty. But despite the bare walls, a strong feeling of warmth and tenderness resonated within the small place.

Love was a difficult emotion to define.

When it came to Prudence, he knew he felt an intense craving that amounted to a lustful desire to bed her. But it was more than that. He yearned to be near her, to hear her opinion on matters of interest, to know she respected him. For her, he wanted to be the best version of himself he could be. Her happiness had suddenly become more important to him than his own.

Good Lord, he really had bested his father this time. The bastard would spend many restless years in Hell, incensed to find his son had fallen in love with the woman he would make his wife.

∽

Other than visiting her sisters and grandfather, Prue spent

the rest of the day in her room. She had no desire to see Mrs Beecham wandering the corridors. Nor did she feel particularly keen to speak to Max.

Mrs Harris had called in to inform her that dinner would be later than usual as the party had still not returned from Tonbridge. Not that it mattered to Prue. It would be an awkward affair. She still didn't know how she felt about marrying a man who needed a bride to claim his inheritance.

Lost in thoughtful contemplation, the light rap on the door made her jump. Prue climbed down from the bed. Perhaps Max's mistress had called to apologise in a desperate bid to stay.

"I haven't seen you all day," Helena said as Prue opened the door. "I wanted to see if you were in good spirits after what happened this morning."

"Please, come in." Prue stepped back for Helena to enter. "Sit down." Prue sat on the bed while Helena dragged the stool out from under the dressing table. "I couldn't bear to see Mrs Beecham and so decided to stay in here. Has the woman left for London?"

Helena pursed her lips and shook her head. "I've not seen her since breakfast. But her room is opposite ours, and I believe she has spent the day in there. Max told Lucas that she is leaving as soon as the party returns from Tonbridge."

"Well, that is a relief." Prue sighed. Just hearing of Max made her heart flutter. While she was pleased she knew the truth about the inheritance, she had enjoyed frolicking in ignorant bliss. "I thought he cared for me," she suddenly blurted. "I thought he wanted to marry me because of the intense passion we share, and because he enjoys my company. It is a shock to discover marriage means nothing to him other than a means for financial gain."

"I don't believe that." Helena came and sat next to her on the bed. "If you search your heart, you will know the truth.

You have fallen in love with him. And he has most definitely fallen in love with you."

Prue smiled weakly. "But you must admit I have cause to doubt him."

"Trust me. When you are in his arms again, there will be no doubt in your mind." Helena tapped her affectionately on the arm. "Besides, he told Lucas how he feels about you. You need to hear it from Max's lips, not mine. But I think when he declares himself you will be overjoyed."

Had Max developed an affection for her? After their amorous interludes outdoors, she felt she would die if she couldn't feel his scorching lips on hers again. "Can I ask you a question? It's about ... well, it's about the passion I spoke of earlier. You do not have to answer."

Helena chuckled as excitement flashed in her eyes. "Oh, please ask away."

Prue could feel a blush rise to her cheeks. As the eldest, she had no one to speak to of such things. "When we ... when ... oh, I am too embarrassed to say it."

"You're speaking of the time you spent in the maze with Max yesterday. When you did a little more than search for the exit."

Prue gasped as her warm cheeks flamed. "You saw us?"

Helena smiled. "Only from my window. I was looking for Lucas. I watched you walk into the maze together." She raised a coy brow. "Indeed, I spent an hour in there with Lucas after dinner, so I know how being hidden amidst the topiary might seem so wickedly enticing. We do not have a maze at home, but now I think Lucas is desperate to find a place in the garden where he might plant one."

Prue recalled their earlier discussion about spending time outdoors, and her comments suddenly conveyed a whole new meaning.

"I did what you suggested," Prue said. "I was simply

myself, and then things became a little heated. Is it usual to be consumed by one's passion to the point of madness?"

"There is nothing more satisfying than being deliriously in love to the point you forget anyone or anything else exists."

Prue considered Helena's words. Was it a delirious love or a ravaging lust clawing away inside? Perhaps it was a beautiful concoction of the two.

"My advice is simple," Helena continued. "Forget about the inheritance. Go to him. Tell him how you feel. Give yourself over to these scandalous desires, safe in the knowledge that the gentleman will be your husband. Use your womanly wiles to make him want you all the more, and I guarantee you will both be eternally happy."

Helena made an illicit liaison sound wonderful.

Prue had spent the last two years being the dependable one. She'd had no time for doubts and insecurities and refused to play the insipid damsel in distress. Helena was right. She would be honest with him, seduce him to the point of madness so she would never have a need to doubt him again.

CHAPTER 11

Prue changed and tidied her hair before going in search of Max. She wore the dress Madame Duval had designed as she liked the way the lord's gaze often dipped to admire the bodice. It made her feel confident as a woman, and she needed something to bolster her courage.

Overcome with a sudden rush of excitement at the thought of being alone with Max, she almost missed the note on the floor near the door. Picking it up and turning it over, she noticed her name written clearly on the front. It was not sealed, and so she peeled back the folds and read the few scrawled lines.

It appeared Max wished to talk to her away from the house. As the party had recently arrived home from Tonbridge, he suggested the maze would be the best place to afford them some privacy.

Prue's heart soared when she saw that Max had signed off with an affectionate endearment. With a quick glance out of the window, she noted the garden was empty. Soon, the tired guests would come to rest in their rooms until dinner, and she did not wish to give anyone cause to gossip about her motives for loitering behind the hedgerow.

As she made her way downstairs, she could hear excited chatter spilling out of the drawing room. They must have been in desperate need of refreshments which gave her more time to slip out unnoticed.

Although it was still light outside, the height of the topiary hedges made the maze feel quite dark and oppressive. Prue didn't know whether to linger near the entrance or wander to the secluded recess, to the spot where she had almost given herself to the man she still hoped to marry. Hearing the crunch of booted footsteps on the gravel path, she decided to play another game.

"This way," she called, waiting to see a brief glimpse of a coat and breeches before turning the corner at the end of the narrow aisle. She raced around and hid in the recess, waited until she heard the steps heading towards her before jumping out. "Caught you," she chuckled, throwing her arms around the lord in the same way he had done to her the day before.

But her arms were not long enough to stretch around the broad chest filling her vision.

"When Catrina spoke of your fascination with me, she never mentioned you'd be so eager for my company."

Prue glanced up to lock gazes with Lord Mannerly. "My lord," she panted as he wrapped his arms around her and backed her into the recess. "I'm afraid there has been some mistake, some terrible misunderstanding."

Lord Mannerly's licentious gaze raked over her. "Catrina said you like to play games. Some ladies find my height intimidating, but she assured me you enjoy the hard, masterful approach. If only you had made your feelings known sooner, we could have had a hell of a weekend. Instead, you had to invite me out here, when we could have enjoyed the comforts of a bed."

"I did not invite you," she yelled. Lord Mannerly had arms the width of any normal gentleman's thighs, and she wriggled and struggled to break free from his grasp. "If you will just let me go so I can explain."

"Don't be embarrassed," he whispered, lowering his head. The sickly smell of some foul spice flooded her nostrils, and she turned her head sharply, desperate to breathe fresh air. "Catrina told me you have no hope of being wed at your age and so often seek ways to have discreet liaisons."

Discreet liaisons?

There was only one man Prue wanted to dally with, and it certainly wasn't Lord Mannerly. "That woman is a lying, conniving old crone." Mrs Beecham's behind had better be wobbling all the way back to London else Prue would happily hang for murder.

"Are you to keep up your delightful act throughout our encounter? While I find it rather arousing now, I fear it might become tiresome quite quickly. A gentleman wants to feel a lady is enjoying the experience after all."

It appeared Lord Mannerly was a dolt, a dunce, and a dullard.

"I doubt my betrothed will take kindly to your wandering hands, my lord." Prue stamped on his toe. But his feet were so large, his boots so hard, that the oaf never felt a thing.

"Your betrothed," he scoffed. "Pray give me the name of this fictitious gentleman so that I may ready my pistols and meet him on the common at dawn."

The lord mimicked the dramatic intonation of a Shakespearean actor from an amateur play.

Good heavens.

"I am betrothed to Lord Roxbury, you imbecile." Prue glared at him, and he made a silly face back.

"Now I know this is part of your charade," Mannerly mocked. He gave a loud chuckle. "Everyone knows he is set to wed your pretty sister. Why on earth do you think he gathered us all here if not to make a declaration?"

Prue saw no point in trying to reason with the man, and so gave a long exasperated sigh before clenching her teeth. "Get your damn hands off me before I scream."

Lord Mannerly raised an arrogant brow. "If that is your way of telling me to cover your mouth with my own, then I am only too happy to oblige," he said as he lowered his head.

∽

Max was in the drawing room, listening to Mrs Shelby's account of Wise's Tunbridge Ware showroom where she had spotted a delightful wooden box. Thankfully, Mrs Harris rescued him from the tiring recount, insisting she speak to him in the hall.

"Mrs Beecham is all set to leave, my lord."

Thank heavens.

"Where is she now?" he asked, feeling a strange sense of trepidation. He would feel much more relaxed knowing she was out of the house.

Mrs Harris did not have a chance to answer as Catrina came stomping down the stairs. Aware of a certain awkwardness, his housekeeper inclined her head before scuttling away quietly.

"Well, I wish I could say it has been a pleasure, Max." Catrina stuck her nose in the air as she came to stand in front of him. "But you're far too stuffy of late, and I find your company equally tiresome. Let us part as friends. Let me wish you well in your pursuit of happiness. I am certain you're going to need it."

Max sighed. He was tired of listening to her sly, resentful remarks. "Trench will take you back to London. I estimate it will be somewhere near midnight when you roll into the city, and so I suggest you do not delay your departure a moment longer."

Catrina offered an arrogant smirk as she thrust her fingers into her gloves. Despite her air of indifference, he could hear her grinding her teeth. "I hope you enjoy being a cuckold, Max. I have it on good authority you're not the only gentleman Miss Roxbury admires. It appears your maze is quite the draw when it comes to entertainment."

Before he could demand an explanation for her cryptic comment, Lucas suddenly appeared. "There you are. You must come with me and be quick."

Catrina chuckled. "Oh, dear. Has something awful happened?"

Max narrowed his gaze. He could tell by her satisfied grin she had been up to mischief. He took a step closer. "What the bloody hell have you done?"

"Forget about her," Lucas commanded. "She is not important."

Max glared at Catrina. "Make sure you're gone by the time I return." He followed Lucas out into the garden, tried to keep up with his friend's long strides. "What is it? Is it Miss Roxbury?"

"Helena saw Miss Roxbury head into the maze," Lucas said with a sigh. "Less than a minute or so later, Lord Mannerly followed her. Helena refused to wait until I had found you and rushed off down the hall."

"Bloody hell! But Mannerly's not the sort to force himself on a lady." Had Catrina not roused his suspicion with her bitter remarks, he would have believed the event to be nothing more than a coincidence. "Catrina has obviously had a hand in orchestrating a scene to discredit Miss Roxbury's reputation. As if other people's opinions matter to me."

"If things are as they appear, I think Mrs Beecham simply wanted to cause Miss Roxbury some distress. After all, who would have known they were out here. With the other guests taking refreshments in the drawing room, there would have been no witnesses."

The thought of Prue struggling against a giant of a man like Mannerly caused Max to break into a run. Anger flared. He was annoyed with himself for not going to speak to her sooner, for not insisting Catrina left the moment she had sauntered into his home uninvited.

As soon as they entered the maze, they heard a woman's cries and a man's deep groaning. They ran along the network of paths until they came to the secluded recess; the place where he had kissed Prue the day before. It took a moment for Max's mind to absorb the strange scene unfolding before him.

Lord Mannerly lay in a heap on the floor. Prue's grandfather sat astride him, clutching his coat lapels and shaking the distressed lord into submission. Helena Dempsey stood over them, prodding the lord's arm with the sharp point of a black umbrella.

"If he so much as raises a brow, hit him, Mrs Dempsey." Her grandfather glared at the terrified gentleman. "That's what scoundrels deserve."

"Oh, I certainly will," Helena Dempsey said with a chuckle as she prodded Lord Mannerly. "Shame on you, my lord."

Prue stood behind them, her hand resting on her chest as she gasped for breath. Max stared at her. His heart swelled; his soul soared. Their gazes locked, and he held out his arms. The simple gestured conveyed all there was to say. Prue skirted around the body on the floor and rushed over to him.

"Captain Lawrence," her grandfather declared. "You're just in time. Take this good-for-nothing blackguard and lock him up."

Max wrapped his arms around Prue and hugged her tightly.

"Have you caught the spy, Mr Hargrove?" Lucas asked in his feigned military manner.

The old man shook his head. "I'm afraid not, Captain. But this blighter is guilty of threatening to ruin a lady's reputation. He'll need ten lashes for his trouble."

"Or a couple more prods with an umbrella," Helena said eagerly.

"For heaven's sake," Mannerly implored. "It is all a terrible misunderstanding. Tell them, Miss Roxbury. Tell them what Mrs Beecham told me. Tell them about the note. Good Lord, the lady has already kneed me in the groin and twisted my nose."

"I don't care what you think you were about," the old man yelled as he shook the lord a few more times, "gentlemen do not accost ladies in the shrubbery."

Lucas coughed into his fist as Helena turned and gave him a coquettish smirk.

Max smiled. "I'm certain husbands are allowed to be more adventurous," he whispered to his friend.

Prue looked up at him. "Where does that leave you, my lord?" She stood on the tips of her toes and whispered, "How do you account for your amorous antics in the shrubbery?"

Max caressed her cheek. "I am a husband in training. It grants me leave to experiment. Come. Let us go and discuss the matter somewhere a little more private."

"I know just the place." Her seductive tone caused desire to flare.

"What would you like me to do with Lord Mannerly?" Max glanced down at the helpless giant. He was guilty of being used as a pawn by a woman intent on causing misery. He was guilty of stupidity. "Shall I throw him out?"

Prue shook her head. "No. Catrina did an excellent job of

persuading him of my affections. You should have seen his face when Grandpapa and Helena charged at him. He may be a giant, but he looked like a terrified mouse."

Max turned to Lucas. "What do you say, Captain? Shall we take Mannerly inside and administer his punishment?"

Mannerly's eyes widened in horror. "Please, Miss Roxbury. Tell them to show mercy."

Lucas folded his arms across his chest and raised an arrogant brow. "I have just the thing in mind. Mannerly will spend the duration of the evening in the company of Mrs Shelby."

Max chuckled. He'd rather jump into a pen of starving pigs. "A splendid idea. She can tell you all about her collection of wooden boxes. It's fascinating. Absolutely thrilling."

Mannerly groaned. "I'd prefer ten lashes and twenty pokes with an umbrella."

Prue took her grandfather's arm, helped him up and hugged him.

"What's that for, girl?" he said with a chuckle.

"For coming to my rescue," she replied affectionately. "For always being there to protect me."

Max helped Mannerly to his feet, brushed the dirt from his coat, and through gritted teeth whispered, "Lay a hand on my wife again, and not even your family will be able to recognise you."

"Forgive me, Roxbury," Mannerly begged. "I thought you wanted the golden-haired one. But I swear to you, I shall make amends for my utter lack of judgement."

"Damn right you will. I am certain you can find a way to compensate Miss Roxbury for all you have done." Indeed, the gentleman could start by telling everyone he knew what a charming lady he found Sarah Roxbury to be.

"I'll do anything."

"Good." Max laughed to himself. "We shall all go inside and wait with bated breath while you ask Mrs Shelby to describe, in great detail, the box she saw at Wise's today."

They all walked back to the house. Upon entering the drawing room, they were pleased to find Mrs Beecham had departed. They were equally surprised to find a new arrival.

"Anthony," Max marched over to his friend who was talking to Sarah Roxbury and Aunt Gwendoline. "Where on earth have you been?"

"Lord Harwood was delayed with estate business," his aunt informed before Anthony could even open his mouth, "and has only just managed to drag himself away."

Lucas came over and patted his brother affectionately on the back. "We missed you," he said. "I was beginning to think you were avoiding me."

"I would have been here sooner, but ... well, I shall not bore you with the details."

"You're here now," Sarah said, her wide smile causing Anthony to suck in a breath. "That's all that matters. And you have not missed very much."

Max turned to look at Prue. "No, it's been a rather quiet affair. Let me introduce Miss Prudence Roxbury, soon to be Lady Roxbury and my wife."

His aunt put a hand on her chest. "What is this? You tell the world before your own aunt."

"Forgive me, Aunt," Max said. "I'm afraid excitement, and the fact I am thoroughly besotted, has addled my brain."

His aunt kissed them both and all the guests took it in turns to offer their heartfelt congratulations.

Max waited for an opportunity to sneak away with Prue. There were things he wanted to say, many things he wanted to do. Just when he thought they had a chance to escape, Helena came over to them.

"Is it my imagination or is Anthony staring at your sister

as though she is the most delicious dish he has ever seen?" Helena touched Prue on the arm. "I have never seen him look so enthralled with a lady."

Max glanced at his friend, who had not left Sarah Roxbury's side since making her acquaintance. "I have never known Anthony to express an interest in any particular lady. Indeed, he is usually quite a private, reserved gentleman."

Helena gasped. "Did you see that? His gaze fell to her lips and lingered there for far too long. Oh, wait until I mention it to Lucas."

"Sarah seems more than happy to keep him company," Prue added.

"We shall have to arrange another meeting." Helena pursed her lips and narrowed her gaze. "Perhaps we could all go to London for a week, help things along a little. Anthony always has business matters to attend to, and we will take our son George whom he adores."

Max shook his head. "I'm certain Anthony is capable of wooing a lady without our interference."

"You don't understand," Helena implored. "He is so terribly lonely. I just know it. And he has been so distant of late. He has not been out in society for months. He avoids all complications and needs someone to intervene."

Prue turned to him. "I know your aunt promised to act as Sarah's chaperone and she still can, but once we're married our support can only help matters."

Max groaned inwardly. He had hoped to spend some quiet time in the country, have Prue all to himself. "I suppose a couple of days won't hurt. We would not want to leave your grandfather and sisters for too long."

Prue nodded. "We will discuss it after dinner. It will give me a chance to gauge Sarah's reaction when we speak about Lord Harwood."

Helena gave a satisfied sigh. "Excellent. Now, I have taken up far too much of your time, and I know I stopped you both from sneaking out." She gestured to the door. "Quick, you can go now. Should anyone notice, I shall pretend to swoon."

CHAPTER 12

"Where are we going?" Max asked. "I assumed we would find somewhere quiet outside."

Prue gripped his hand and pulled him along the hallway towards the study. "I know of a much better place." Her stomach fluttered at the thought of being alone with him. She would follow Helena's advice: she would give herself over to her scandalous desires, safe in the knowledge Max would soon be her husband.

She opened the door to his study and locked it behind them.

"I see," he said with a wicked grin. "You wish to continue what we began in here last night."

"I wish to explore a new avenue." She wasn't sure how she found the breath to speak. Blood pulsed through her veins at far too rapid a rate. "In the secret room, we are guaranteed privacy."

She pushed the panel that opened into the snug. Max followed her inside and closed the concealed door. Although the walls were bare, she still felt an overwhelming sense of love envelop her. She was pleased to see he had removed the furniture as the space would prove useful for what she had in mind.

"I thought to gift you the chair and table. I meant to tell you two weeks ago when you came to give me a tour of the estate, but I had other things on my mind."

"That's very generous. I don't know what your plans are for the room, but I think you should leave it empty. For me, this place has always been about love." Her throat grew tight as she spoke. She turned to face him and pushed her hands up over his chest. "Whenever you think about the first time I told you I love you, I want you to remember this moment. I want your mind to conjure images that will be forever locked in this room."

"Was that a declaration, Miss Pickle?" Max said, pulling her into his arms. "And you still haven't told me why your family call you that."

"It's rather silly and not a very interesting story. I love being tickled. As a child, I struggled to say the word. My parents thought it rather endearing, and so it stuck."

His lips curled into a sinful smile. "And where do you like to be tickled, Miss Pickle?"

"All over my body, my lord."

"Do you know how excited I am at the prospect of testing the theory?" He cupped her cheek. "Am I forgiven, Prue? You must know by now that I would give everything I own just for the chance to marry you. You must know I'm in love with you."

Her heart soared. "I love you," she whispered. She had been so afraid of her feelings, yet the truth shone from her so bright and beautiful. "Let us continue what we started in the maze."

Max glanced at the floor. "What? Here?"

Her chest felt full and warm, the pulsing between her legs needed his touch. "Right here, right now."

When his eyes widened, she saw her own desire reflected there. "What is it that you want?"

"I want everything you have to give." Her voice sounded sultry, not at all like her. She undid the bow at the back of her dress. "Won't you help me with the buttons?"

He swallowed visibly. "Good God, Prue, I doubt I can stop my blasted fingers from shaking."

She chuckled, the sound soon turning into breathless pants and moans as they stripped each other naked.

Prue glanced down at his hard body with a look of shock and wonder. "The first time I came to see you, I said I needed something of monumental proportion. It appears I was not mistaken."

He raised an arrogant brow. "And I told you I had plenty to give."

She gasped. "Is that what you meant?"

"Prue, I wanted you from the moment I saw you wrestling with a plant pot. I fell in love with you that day, too."

"And I have loved you since you threw your friend out for insulting me."

Max took her hand and lowered her down on top of the mound of discarded garments. "I shall try to be mindful of your situation," he said, coming to lie on top of her, "but I'm so desperate to be inside you, I fear the moment may be over in minutes."

The weight of his warm body sent her thoughts scattering. "We'll have a lifetime to practice, to take things slow. Make me yours, Max. Do it now."

From the growl resonating in his throat, she'd said something right.

Without further ado, he devoured her mouth, rained kisses along her jaw, down to her breasts. He took her nipple into his mouth, each lick of his tongue sending bolts of desire shooting to her core.

Prue threaded her fingers through his hair, tugged and pulled to force him to continue.

"Bloody hell," he muttered breaking for breath. "At this rate, I'll not last a minute."

Max rolled on to his side, stroked the sensitive place between her legs until she was panting, begging for more. Sliding his finger inside her, he sucked in a breath. "God, you're so warm, so wet. Damn, I feel as though I've waited forever to touch you like this."

Leaning over to claim her mouth again, he rolled on top of her. The feel of his solid shaft pressed against her belly caused liquid fire to pool in her most intimate place.

"Don't wait any longer, Max."

"I don't intend to."

He nudged her thighs wider apart and settled between them. Prue wrapped her legs around him, felt his impressive manhood push into her body. The first few thrusts were slow, measured. But then in one fluid movement, he filled her full.

"Max," Prue cried out, but the fleeting pang quickly subsided.

"I'm sorry."

"Don't be," she said breathlessly, gripping his buttocks as he withdrew and entered her again and again in a seductive rhythm.

Prue hugged him tight with every muscle and fibre of her being. She felt connected to him in a way she'd never dreamed possible. An ache, a desperate yearning burst to life in her core. When he rocked his hips, and his powerful thrusts grew more frantic, she felt herself edging towards something magnificent.

"Oh, God." Her world shattered as her body pulsed, shook and drew him deeper.

A guttural groan escaped from his lips as he stilled for a second, slid inside her one last time and stayed there.

"Bloody hell." Max leant down and pressed a chaste kiss to her lips. "We need to marry as soon as I can get a licence. Damn, I'll not wait for the banns to be read before having you again."

"You don't have to wait. We can come in here whenever the mood takes us."

Max collapsed on to his back and grinned. "What, you'll make the two-mile journey twice a day?"

"Twice a day?" she said with some surprise, but her stomach performed a flip at the prospect of taking him into her body again.

"Now I've found you, I don't intend to let you go." He put his arm around her and gathered her close. "I've instructed repairs to be made to the tower, and then we'll have two secret places to indulge our desires."

Prue struggled to hide her excitement and her body still tingled with sated passion. "Oh, Max, it will be wonderful. We'll have our own woodland den where we can stay the night."

"I agree, it will be wonderful as I have no intention of sleeping once we're in there."

She ran her hand over his chest as she lay at his side. "After what has just occurred, I have no intention of sleeping, either."

He chuckled. "You know how to tease a man, Miss Pickle." He glanced around the room. "What about dinner? I have lost all concept of time. Perhaps we should head upstairs to wash and change."

She didn't want to be anywhere else other than in his arms. "With Lord Harwood arriving, I doubt anyone will miss us. Perhaps we could stay here."

"Prue, I'm the host. Of course they will miss us."

With her hand resting on his chest, she decided to be a little more adventurous. Suppressing her nerves, she ran the tips of her fingers over the muscles in his abdomen. "Are you sure you don't want to stay here?" The same fingers moved to caress the tops of his thighs. "Are you sure I cannot persuade you to be late for dinner?"

The most fascinating part of his anatomy twitched in response, and he growled as he rolled on top of her. "How can I resist such a tempting offer? As I am mindful that you may need a little time to recover from my masterful claiming, perhaps we could explore other avenues, as you suggested."

"What did you have in mind?"

"You'll see."

They were inexcusably late for dinner.

Max explained that it had all been part of the night's entertainment. They were acting as survivors of a shipwreck, suffering from terrible memory loss and consequently could not find their way to the dining room. With an air of frustration, he complained that his guests had failed in their task to find them, despite the numerous hints he had given throughout the day.

"I recall you did look rather vacant when I described my Tunbridge Ware," Mrs Shelby said. Her eyes suddenly grew wide. "Yes. You said you had forgotten that wooden boxes could be so fascinating."

"Indeed," Mr Wyebourne uttered. "Many times I have noticed you put your fingers to your temples and sway."

Helena Dempsey assured everyone that it was a game played in all the best houses. "I think they have excelled in their efforts to put on a convincing show," she said patting her gloved hands in applause. "They have not even changed for dinner. Looking at their crumpled attire, how could one not believe they have been rolling around on deck?"

The End

Thank you!

Thank you for reading
What Every Lord Wants.

Reviews helps readers find books. If you enjoyed this book please consider letting people know by leaving a brief review on Amazon.

Would you like to know what happened when Sarah Roxbury met Anthony Dempsey in London?

Turn the page to read an excerpt from

The Secret to Your Surrender.

THE SECRET TO YOUR SURRENDER

Adele Clee

All he wanted was to safeguard his secret.

All she wanted was his surrender.

CHAPTER 1

Anthony Dempsey, fifth Viscount Harwood, jumped up from the chair behind his mahogany desk and glared at his brother, Lucas. "Do you not think it appropriate to knock before you barge into a gentleman's study?"

"No. Not when I have had to drag myself away from Lord Daleforth's ball to come and search for you." Dressed immaculately in evening attire, Lucas folded his arms across his chest. "Are you not prepared to offer an explanation? Are you ill? Did you have a prior engagement you failed to mention?"

Anthony suppressed a sigh. "I had every intention of attending this evening." The lie fell easily from his lips though it left a bitter aftertaste that would taint his palate for hours. He gestured to the pile of papers scattered over the desk. "I simply lost all concept of time."

Lucas raised a dubious brow. "You are, or at least you were, the most reliable person I know." He shrugged. "Is it Miss Roxbury? Do you not wish to spend time in her company?"

The mere mention of her name roused an image of a

CHAPTER 1

golden-haired goddess — a luscious, tempting beauty with the power to make a man lose his mind.

"I find her fascinating, utterly beguiling." That was not a lie. One glance and she had held him captive. "I've not the time nor the inclination to wed. It would be wrong to allow her to think otherwise."

"You no longer believe it is your duty to beget an heir?" Lucas asked incredulously.

Securing the family's heritage was a responsibility Anthony took seriously. He refused to be the foolish peer who let title and wealth cultivated through many generations slip through his fingers.

"You are my heir. Your son will one day be a viscount. Does the thought not please you?" He knew the answer to his question before noting Lucas' look of disdain.

Lucas gave an indolent wave. "Trust me. I do not regard it a blessing. How could I when you are shackled to your desk with no hope of reprieve?"

"I was born to shoulder responsibility." Duty, both the legal and moral obligation to one's family, was his birthright. "It is all I know."

"You are allowed some pleasure." Lucas stepped closer. "I want you to be happy. I do not want to walk in here and find a lonely, withered old man hunched over his desk."

Anthony chuckled though he found nothing amusing about his situation. "I have more than a few years before my eyesight fails me and my hair turns grey."

"Come with me," Lucas implored. "I shall wait while you change. Make your position clear to Miss Roxbury and enjoy her company as a friend."

A friend?

Friendship required a level of affection beyond his capabilities. In Miss Roxbury's company, he often found himself lost in wistful dreams of a dark, all-consuming passion, of a life filled with love and laughter.

"It is far too late to contemplate attending now," he said, his excuse feeble.

Lucas jerked his head back. "It is but ten o'clock. We'll arrive in plenty of time for supper."

"I will meet with you tomorrow."

There was a prolonged moment of silence.

"Helena begged me to come." Lucas' tone held a confidence in his ability to sway Anthony's decision. "I know how you hate to disappoint her. She will not sleep tonight unless she sees you and knows you are well."

Bloody hell!

His brother was a master of strategy and knew to wait to play his trump card.

"Your constant refusal to attend social functions is making her ill with worry," Lucas continued. "She fears you are suffering from an incurable malady and are attempting to avoid discovery."

"I am not ill," Anthony replied, knowing he was but seconds away from surrender. "I am sure you will find a way to placate her."

Lucas cast a look of reproach. "If that is what you wish me to tell her upon my return then so be it."

Age and position may have placed Anthony as head of the family, but Helena was the one who nurtured relationships. Since their mother's passing, Helena was the one who worked to strengthen bonds.

Guilt pricked his conscience.

In one respect, he supposed he *was* suffering from a malady. His secret was akin to a debilitating affliction that rendered him helpless. It lay buried inside the empty cavern of his chest, robbed him of all rational thought.

If he revealed the truth, Helena would berate him for his

dishonesty. There was every chance she would not trust him again, her disappointment evident in her tone and manner whenever their paths crossed.

"You use your wife to force my hand. What next? No doubt little George is waiting in the hall with his nursemaid, a look of disappointment swimming in his eyes because his uncle has upset his mama."

An arrogant smile played at the corners of Lucas' mouth. "Damn. You know me so well."

He should have told Lucas to go to the devil, but he owed Helena a debt of gratitude that far outweighed the need to prove a point. Equally, it would not be wise to rouse her suspicions further. For a fleeting moment, he considered telling Lucas the truth but shook the idea away, along with the thought of spending a quiet night at home.

"Give me fifteen minutes," Anthony said as he strode to the door of his study. "And pour me a large glass of brandy while you wait."

He would need something to rid his mind of his pressing problems. Brandy would prove to be a far less complicated distraction than losing himself in Miss Roxbury's alluring gaze.

∼

After paying his respects to Lord Daleforth and offering an apology for his late arrival, Anthony followed Lucas and went in search of Helena and her companions, the Roxburys.

They located Max Roxbury on the outskirts of the ballroom conversing with his wife Prudence while Helena sat in a chair only a foot away.

"Ah, the elusive Lord Harwood has appeared at last," Max said with a hint of amusement as he cast Anthony a sidelong glance.

CHAPTER 1

"It would not do to be too predictable," Anthony replied. "But in truth, I was waylaid with matters relating to estate business."

They did not need to raise their chins, twitch their brows or mutter between themselves for him to know they found his excuse far from convincing.

Lucas barged past them and crouched at Helena's side. "Are you well? You look pale." He stared into her eyes. "Perhaps you should have stayed at home this evening."

Anthony sighed. His brother was intent on proving his point.

"Nonsense." She gave an indolent wave and a weak chuckle. "I am tired that is all. But I did not want to miss the opportunity to spend time with my brother."

Guilt surfaced.

"Forgive me," Anthony said, coming to stand before her. He took Helena's gloved hand and brought it to his lips. "The last thing I want is to cause you distress."

Helena smiled. "Well, you are here now, though I am afraid Miss Roxbury grew tired of waiting and in your absence has taken to the dance floor."

Prudence cleared her throat. "Indeed. My sister is dancing with the Earl of Barton."

Barton? A frisson of fear coursed through Anthony's veins.

Despite all efforts to the contrary, it took but a few seconds for his gaze to drift to the couples gliding gracefully about the floor. It took but one glance for him to locate the lady who often plagued his dreams.

As though drawn by an undefinable force, he turned and took a few steps towards the open display of merriment.

Sarah Roxbury's golden hair shimmered in the candlelight as she swirled around the floor. Her cheeks were pink, flushed from exertion. Joy and happiness oozed from every fibre of her being, the fiery glow setting her apart from every other woman in the room. As did her smile, for it was pure, natural, free from artifice. Dazzling.

The muscles in his abdomen grew taut, tight. While lust clawed at his flesh like a savage beast, another emotion took precedence.

Jealousy.

The Earl of Barton held Sarah Roxbury's gloved hand in a talon-like grip. His beady stare dropped to the swell of smooth, creamy flesh visible above the neckline of her gown.

Anthony growled, albeit silently.

The need to claim the only woman he had ever wanted, pushed to the fore. Murderous thoughts swamped him. His knuckles throbbed as he imagined landing a hard punch on the pompous lord's jaw. Though he considered the Earl of Barton an acquaintance, he was one of five gentlemen on Anthony's list of suspects.

Damn it all. He should not have come.

Lucas hovered at his side. "Standing there glaring will only add weight to the theory you have claimed Miss Roxbury for yourself."

Anthony snorted. "That sounds familiar. I recall saying the same thing to you once."

"Yes, and I married the lady in question."

"I do not intend to marry Miss Roxbury," Anthony whispered through gritted teeth. With the complicated nature of his problems, he could not marry anyone.

"You want her. It is blatantly obvious."

Were his feelings so transparent?

He was a man in control of his emotions. Exaggerated displays of sentiment left one vulnerable, open to ridicule. In such cases, honesty proved challenging.

Anthony brushed his hand through his hair. "We cannot always have what we want."

CHAPTER 1

"You are speaking to the wrong man if you're looking for sympathy. I see nothing other than pathetic excuses standing in your way."

Lucas would not feel the same way if he knew of the recent developments at Elton Park.

The music came to an end. The couples smiled and conversed as they took a moment to catch their breath. Anthony stared at Barton, studied every facial expression, every nuance, searching for clues.

What were his intentions towards Miss Roxbury?

Was he the one guilty of committing the heinous crimes?

Barton inclined his head to him as he edged past to escort Miss Roxbury back to the safety of her family.

"Ah, Harwood." The earl tapped him on the upper arm. "I have not seen you since that rather entertaining little gathering you had last year."

Was the gentleman trying to provoke him?

"I have been preoccupied of late," Anthony confessed. It took all his strength not to lock gazes with Miss Roxbury, yet he could feel her penetrating stare searching his face.

"I must thank you again, Lord Barton, for such a delightful turn about the floor." Miss Roxbury's flirtatious tone drifted through the air. Rather than soothe or excite it roused Anthony's ire.

"The pleasure was all mine," Barton replied in a sly, slippery way that revealed the lascivious nature of his thoughts. "Indeed, if you are not otherwise engaged, you may mark me down for another dance of your choosing."

Lucas coughed discreetly into his fist and raised a mocking brow.

Anthony swallowed down the hard lump beating wildly in his throat. Damn it all. The urge to punch the Earl of Barton took hold. Indeed, the ends of his fingers tingled and pulsed. His vision blurred. Harrowing images bombarded his mind: a golden-haired beauty protesting at the scoundrel's wandering hands, her screaming for help though no one could hear.

"I am certain I have space on my card," Miss Roxbury replied.

The first few strains of a waltz filtered through the hum of lively conversation. Fearing the earl would be bold enough to request his second dance immediately, Anthony stepped forward.

He held out his hand to her. "I believe if you examine your card you will find the next dance is mine, Miss Roxbury." The arrogant, rather rakish undercurrent to his tone was so unlike him.

To quash the thrum of desire, he told himself his motive for dancing was purely logical. The Earl of Barton could well be a murderous rogue intent on making even more mischief. Anthony valued Max Roxbury's friendship too much to place his wife's sister in danger.

Miss Roxbury's beguiling blue eyes focused on his hand.

There was a moment of silence. Anthony sensed her hesitation, wondered if she would call him to task for being so presumptuous.

When she inclined her head, all muscles in his body tensed to prepare for the internal battle soon to commence.

"I am surprised you remembered." Miss Roxbury's tone conveyed a hint of reproof. "You appear to be so forgetful of late."

She placed her dainty hand in his. Nothing prepared him for the sudden rush of excitement. Nothing prepared him for the desperate pangs of longing pounding in his chest.

For the first time in his life, he wished he was his brother: a man with the strength and conviction to follow his heart. He wished he was a man without the crippling complications that would inevitably lead to a life of loneliness.

CHAPTER 1

Suppressing a heavy sigh, he led Miss Roxbury out onto the floor, and prayed he would survive the next five minutes. Come first light he would leave London and return to Elton Park. To remain would be akin to torture and he saw no end in sight to this form of self-flagellation.

Where Sarah Roxbury was concerned, it was time to accept Fate had chosen to direct them along different paths.

It was time to stop dreaming.

It was time to accept she could never be his.

Do you want to read more?
The Secret to Your Surrender is available now!

Books by Adele Clee

To Save a Sinner

A Curse of the Heart

What Every Lord Wants

The Secret To Your Surrender

A Simple Case of Seduction

Anything for Love Series

What You Desire

What You Propose

What You Deserve

What You Promised

The Brotherhood Series

Lost to the Night

Slave to the Night

Abandoned to the Night

Lured to the Night

Lost Ladies of London

The Mysterious Miss Flint

The Deceptive Lady Darby

The Scandalous Lady Sandford

The Daring Miss Darcy

Printed in Great Britain
by Amazon